"How do you know I'm conventional?"

"Oh, please. You can't possibly not be conventional. You showed up at that fire at three thirty in the morning in a neat and completely pressed uniform. You don't believe in hypnotism. Everything about you is conventional."

"Ms. Torres, trust me when I say that you do not know everything about me."

Her eyes met his and he recognized that little weird energy that passed between them. He wished he didn't, but there was no denying the flirtatious undertone to all of this. He should stop it immediately.

But she held his gaze and she smiled. "Natalie. You should call me Natalie, remember?"

That uncomfortable and unwelcome attraction dug deeper into his gut. The kind of deeper that led a man to make foolish mistakes and stupid decisions. The kind he knew better than to indulge in.

But it was also the kind that tended to override that knowledge.

STONE COLD TEXAS RANGER

NICOLE HELM

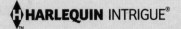
HARLEQUIN INTRIGUE®

To all the episodes of *20/20* and *Dateline* I watched with
my grandma. They might have given me nightmares,
but they also gave me a ton of great book ideas.

ISBN-13: 978-1-335-72075-7

Recycling programs
for this product may
not exist in your area.

Stone Cold Texas Ranger

Copyright © 2016 by Nicole Helm

Printed in U.S.A.

™ www.Harlequin.com

Nicole Helm grew up with her nose in a book and the dream of one day becoming a writer. Luckily, after a few failed career choices, she gets to follow that dream—writing down-to-earth contemporary romance and romantic suspense. From farmers to cowboys, Midwest to *the* West, Nicole writes stories about people finding themselves and finding love in the process. She lives in Missouri with her husband and two sons and dreams of someday owning a barn.

Books by Nicole Helm

Harlequin Intrigue

Stone Cold Texas Ranger

Harlequin Superromance

A Farmers' Market Story

All I Have
All I Am

Falling for the New Guy
Too Friendly to Date
Too Close to Resist

Visit the Author Profile page at Harlequin.com.

CAST OF CHARACTERS

Vaughn Cooper—A Texas Ranger in the Unsolved Crimes Unit. Many of his cases are tied to one mysterious man, known only as The Stallion. He's very suspicious of Natalie Torres as a hypnotist, but when she's in danger, he takes on the responsibility of keeping her safe.

Natalie Torres—A licensed hypnotist who works for the Texas Rangers. When a witness she hypnotized turns up dead and her house is burned down, Natalie must go on the run with Ranger Cooper to keep herself safe.

Gabby Torres—Natalie's sister who disappeared eight years ago and is being kept by The Stallion.

The Stallion/Victor Callihan—A wealthy Texas businessman who is secretly running an organized ring of drugs and trafficking. Most people only know him by his nickname, The Stallion.

Bennet Stevens—Texas Ranger and Vaughn's partner on many cases, including those involving The Stallion. Works the case of Natalie's house fire while Vaughn takes her on the run.

Captain Dean—Head of the Texas Rangers Unsolved Crimes Unit and Vaughn and Bennet's direct supervisor. Often calls in Natalie to hypnotize witnesses for questioning. Sends Vaughn on the run with Natalie.

Jaime Allesandro/Rodriguez—An undercover FBI Agent who has infiltrated The Stallion's crime ring. Real name is Jaime Allesandro; undercover he's known as Rodriguez. The Stallion thinks Rodriguez is helping him find Natalie and Vaughn.

Chapter One

Vaughn Cooper was not an easy man to like. There was a time when he'd been quicker with a smile or a joke, but twelve years in law enforcement and three years in the Unsolved Crimes Investigation Unit of the Texas Rangers had worn off any charm he'd been born with.

He was not a man who believed in the necessity of small talk, politeness or pretending a situation was anything other than what it was.

He was most definitely not a man who believed in *hypnotism*, even if the woman currently putting their witness under acted both confident and capable.

He didn't trust it, her or what she did, and he was more than marginally irritated that the witness seemed to immediately react. No more fidgeting, no more yelling that he didn't know anything. After Natalie Torres's ministrations, the man was still and pleasant.

Vaughn didn't believe it for a second.

"I told you," Bennet Stevens said, giving him a

nudge. Bennet had been his partner for the past two years, and Vaughn liked him. Some days. This was not one of those days.

"It's not real. He's acting." Vaughn made no effort to lower his voice. It was purposeful, and he watched carefully for any sign of reaction from the supposedly hypnotized witness.

He didn't catch any, but he could all but feel Ms. Torres's angry gaze on him. He didn't care if she was angry. All he cared about was getting to the bottom of this case before another woman disappeared.

He wasn't sure his weary conscience could take another thing piled on top of the overflowing heap.

"How are you today, Mr. Herman?" Ms. Torres asked in that light, airy voice she'd hypnotized the man with. Vaughn rolled his eyes. That anyone would fall for this was beyond him. They were police officers. They dealt in evidence and reality, not *hypnotism*.

"Been better," the witness grumbled.

"I see," she continued, that easy, calming tone to her voice never changing. "Can you tell us a little bit about your problems?"

"Nah."

"You know, you're safe here, Mr. Herman. You can speak freely. This is a safe place where you can unburden yourself."

Vaughn tried to tamp down his edgy impatience. He couldn't get over them wasting their time doing this, but it hadn't been his call. This had come from above him, and he had no choice but to follow through.

"Yeah?"

The hypnotist inclined her head toward Vaughn and Bennet. It was the agreed upon sign that they would now take over the questioning.

"It's not a bad gig," Herman said, his hands linked together on the table in front of him. No questions needed.

Yeah, Vaughn didn't believe a second of this.

"Don't have to get my hands too dirty. Paid cash. My old lady's got cancer. Goes a long way, you know?"

"Rough," Bennet said, doing a far better job than Vaughn of infusing some sympathy into his tone. "What kind of jobs you running?"

"Mostly just messages, you know. I don't even gotta be the muscle. Just deliver the information. It's a sweet deal. But…"

"But what?"

Vaughn could feel the hypnotist's eyes on him. Something about her. Something about *this*. It was all off. He wasn't even being paranoid like Bennet too often accused him of. The witness was too easy, and the woman was too jumpy.

"But… Man, I don't like this, though. I got a daughter of my own. I never wanted to get involved with this part."

"What part's that?"

"The girls. He keeps the girls."

Vaughn tensed, and he noticed the hypnotist did, as well.

"Who keeps them?"

Vaughn and Bennet whirled to face Ms. Torres. She wasn't supposed to ask questions. Not after she gave them the signal. Not about the case.

"What the hell do you think—"

"The Stallion," Herman muttered. "But I can't cross The Stallion."

Vaughn immediately looked at Bennet. He gave his partner an imperceptible nod, then Bennet slipped out of the room.

The Stallion. An idiotic name for the head of an organized crime group that had been stealthily wreaking havoc across Texas for ten years. Vaughn had no less than four cases he knew connected to the bastard or his drug-running cronies, but this one...

"What do you know about The Stallion?" Vaughn asked evenly, though frustration pounded in his bloodstream. Still, hypnotism or no hypnotism, he wasn't the type of ranger who let that show.

"You don't cross him. You don't cross him and live."

Vaughn opened his mouth to ask the next question, but the damn hypnotist beat him to it.

"What about the girls?" she demanded, leaning closer. "What do you know about the girls? Where are they?"

Vaughn was so taken aback by her complete disregard for the rules, by her fervent demand, he couldn't say anything at first. But it was only a split second of shock, then he edged his way between Ms. Torres and her line of sight to the witness.

"Get him out," he ordered.

Big brown eyes blinked up at him. "What?"

"If this is hypnotism, unhypnotize him." Vaughn bent over and leaned his mouth close enough to her ear so he could whisper without the witness overhearing. "You are putting my case at risk, and I will not have it. Take him out now, or I'll kick you out."

She didn't waver, and she certainly didn't turn to Herman and take him out. "I'm getting answers," she replied through gritted teeth. Her eyes blazed with righteous fury.

It was no match for his own. Vaughn inclined his head toward Herman, who was shaking his head back and forth. Not offering *any* answers to her too direct line of questioning.

"Mr. Herman—"

Vaughn nudged her chair back with his knee. "Take him out, or I'll arrest you for interfering in a criminal investigation."

Her eyes glittered with that fury, her hands clenched into fists, but when he rested his hand on the handcuffs latched to his utility belt, she closed her eyes.

"Fine, but you need to move."

When she opened her eyes, he saw a weary resignation in her slumped posture, a kind of sorrow in her expression Vaughn didn't understand—didn't want to. Any more than he wanted to figure out what scent she was wearing, because when he was this close to her, it was almost distracting.

Almost.

"If you say one word to him that isn't pulling him out of the hypnotism, you will be arrested. Do you understand?"

"I thought you didn't believe in it?" she snapped.

"I don't, but I'm not going to have you claiming I didn't let you do your job. Take him out. Then you will be talking to my supervisor. Got it?"

She sneered at him, like many a criminal he'd arrested or threatened in his career. He wasn't sure she was a criminal, but he wasn't affected at all by her anger.

She'd ruined the lead. The Stallion wasn't nearly enough to go on, and she'd stepped in with her own reckless, desperate questions, invalidating the whole interrogation.

She was going to pay for this.

NATALIE SAT IN the waiting area of the Unsolved Crimes office. She wanted to fume and rage and pace, but she didn't have time to indulge in pointless anger. Not when she had information to find.

Who was The Stallion? Could this all possibly be

related to her sister? She'd waited three years for this. Three years of dealing with sneering Texas Rangers hating that their higher-ups involved her in their investigations. Three years of hoping against hope that the next case she'd be brought in on would be Gabby's.

Just because the witness had talked about missing girls didn't mean it was her sister's case. As a hypnotist, she was never given any case details, legally bound to secrecy regarding anything she did hear simply by being in the room.

She'd lost her cool. She knew she wasn't supposed to jump in like that, but the interrogators had been asking the wrong questions. They'd been taking too much time. She needed to know. She needed…

She needed not to cry. So, she took a deep breath in, and slowly let it out. She focused on the little window with the blinds closed. Inside, three officers were talking. Probably about her. One definitely complaining about her.

She was angry with herself for breaking rules she knew Texas Rangers weren't going to bend, but she'd rather channel that anger onto Ranger Jerk.

Immature, yes, but the immature nicknames she gave each ranger who gave her a hard time entertained her when she wanted to tell them off.

The problem with Ranger Jerk was she could nearly forget what a jerk he was when he looked like…*that*. He was so tall and broad shouldered, and when he was always crossing his arms over his chest in a threatening manner, it was obvious he had *muscles* underneath the crisp white dress shirt he wore.

Like, the kind of muscles that could probably bench-press *her*. Not that she'd imagined that in those first few minutes of meeting him. Those were flights of fancy she did *not* allow herself. Not on the job.

Then there was his face, which wasn't at all fair. She'd nearly been tongue-tied when he'd greeted her. His darkish blond hair was buzzed short, and his blue eyes were downright mesmerizing. Some light shade that was nearly gray, and she'd spent seconds trying to decide what to call that color.

Until he'd insulted her without a qualm. Because his good looks were only *one* problem with him. Only the tip of the iceberg of problems.

The door opened, and she forced herself to look calm and placid. She was a calm, still lake. No breeze rippled her waters. She reflected nothing but a peaceful and reflective surface.

But maybe a sea monster lurked deep and would leap out of the water and eat all of them in one giant gulp.

Yeah, her imagination had always gotten her into trouble.

"Ms. Torres. Come inside, please."

She held no ill will against Captain Dean. He was one of the few rangers who respected and believed in what she did. He was, more often than not, the one who called her in to help with a case.

But she *had* crossed a line she knew she wasn't supposed to cross, and she was going to have to deal with the consequences—which would gall. For one, because it meant Ranger Jerk got what he wanted. But more important, because she might have finally had some insight into her sister's case, and been too impetuous to make the most of it.

"Have a seat."

She slid into the chair opposite Captain Dean's desk. The two rangers she'd been in the interrogation room with stood on either side.

They were impressive, the three of them. Strong, in control, looking perfectly pressed in what constituted as the Texas Ranger uniform: khakis, a dress shirt and a tie, Ranger badge and belt buckle, topped off with cowboy boots. The only thing the men weren't wearing inside the office were the white cowboy hats.

She wanted to sneer at Ranger Cooper's smug blue eyes, but she didn't. She smiled sweetly instead.

"You breached our contract, Ms. Torres. You know that."

"Yes, sir."

"Your job is not to question witnesses. It's only to put them under hypnosis, should they agree, to calm them and allow us to ask questions."

"I know, sir. I'm sorry for…stepping out of line." She offered both the men who'd been in the room with her the best apologetic smile she could muster. "I got a little carried away. I can promise you, it won't happen again."

"I'm afraid we can't risk second chances at this juncture. Not in this department, not in the Texas Rangers. I'm sorry, Natalie. You've been an asset. But this was unconscionable, and you will not be asked back."

She sat frozen, completely ice from the inside out. *Not be asked back.* But she'd helped solve cases. For years. She'd received a commendation even! And he was...

"Cooper, see her out?"

Ranger Jerk nodded toward the door. "After you."

She swallowed over the lump in her throat. All her chances. All the times she'd been so close to seeing something of Gabby's case. All the *possibility*, and she'd ruined it.

No, *he'd* ruined it for her. *He* had. She stood on shaky legs, clutching her phone and her purse.

"I am sorry."

She didn't look back at Captain Dean, or Ranger Stevens. She didn't want to see the pitying, apologetic looks on their faces. Just like all those other police-men who'd come up with nothing—*nothing* when it came to Gabby's disappearance.

Apologies didn't mean a thing when her sister was gone. Eight years. And Natalie was the only one who held out any hope, and now her hope was...

Well, it had just gotten kicked in the teeth.

She managed to walk stiffly to the door and stepped out, the Jerk of the Manor still behind her. Too close behind her and crowding her out and away.

"I'll see you all the way out of the building, Ms. Torres," he said, sounding so smug and superior.

She walked down the hall, still a little shaken. But shaken had no hold on her anger. She glared at the man striding next to her. "You got me fired, you lousy son of a—"

"I'd reconsider your line of thought and blame, Ms. Torres." He continued to look ahead, not an ounce of emotion showing on his face. "You got yourself fired. Now, stay out of this case. If I catch a whiff of you being involved in it anywhere, I will not hesitate to find out every last thing about you and connect you to whatever dirty deeds you're hiding."

"I am not hiding any dirty deeds." Which was the God's honest truth. She hadn't stepped out of line in eight years. Or ever, really, but especially since Gabby had disappeared.

His eyes met hers, a cold, cold stormy blue. "We'll see."

She shivered involuntarily, because that look made her feel like she *had* done something wrong, which was so absurd.

Even more absurd was the idea of her staying out of the case. She'd take what little information she'd gathered and follow it to the ends of the earth.

Because she refused to believe her sister was dead. A body had never been found, and that Herman man had said…he'd said *he keeps the girls*. Not kept. Not got rid of. *Keeps*.

Maybe Gabby wasn't one of those girls, but it was possible. More than that, she thought. The Texas Rangers might be a mostly good bunch, but they had rules and regulations to follow. Natalie Torres did not.

God help the man who tried to stop her.

Chapter Two

The phone ringing and vibrating on his nightstand jerked Vaughn out of a deep sleep. He cursed and answered it blearily. Phone calls in the middle of the night were never good, but they always had to be answered.

Much to his ex-wife's constant complaints throughout the duration of their marriage.

"Cooper," he grumbled into the speaker.

"You're going to need to get out here."

He recognized his captain's voice immediately. "Text the address."

"Yup."

Vaughn rubbed his hands over his face, then went straight to his closet where a row of work clothes hung, always a few pressed and ready to go. He never liked to be caught without clean and ironed clothes on the ready, even in the middle of the night. He looked at the clock as he dressed. Three fifteen.

He strode through his house, gave the coffeemaker a wistful glance. Even though he always kept it ready to go, he didn't have time to sit around waiting for it to brew. Not at three fifteen.

With a stretch and a groan, he strapped on his gun and tried not to wonder if he was getting too old for this. Thirty-four was hardly too old. He had a lot of years to go before he could take a pension, but more...

He had a lot of cases to solve before his conscience would let him leave. So, he needed to get at it.

He got in his car, and when his phone chimed, he clicked the address Captain Dean had texted and started the GPS directions. It took about fifteen minutes to arrive at his destination, a small neighborhood a little outside the city that he knew was mainly rental houses. Single-storied brick buildings, a few split-levels. Modest homes at best, flat out run-down at worst.

Fire trucks and police vehicles were parked around a burned-out and drowned shell of a house. Though it still smoked, the house had obviously been ravaged by the fire hours earlier.

Vaughn stopped at the barricade, flashed his badge to the officer guarding the perimeter and then went in search of Captain Dean. When he found him, he was with Bennet. Vaughn's uneasy dread grew.

"What've we got?"

"This is the hypnotist's house," Bennet said gravely.

The dread in Vaughn's gut hardened to a rock. The house was completely destroyed, which meant—

"She's fine. She wasn't home, which is lucky for her, because someone was. Herman."

"Dead?"

Captain Dean nodded. "He didn't start and botch the fire, either, at least from what information I've been able to gather. We'll have to wait to go over everything with the fire investigator once she's done, but I think it got back to somebody Herman squealed. Body was dumped."

"The hypnotist? Where was she?"

"With her mom," Bennet offered, "who works at a gas station down on Clark. We've got guys going over surveillance, but so far she's on the tape almost the entire night. She came home just after some neighbors called 9-1-1. She's innocent."

Innocent? Maybe of this, but Natalie Torres was hardly innocent. The day was full of far too much weirdness for her to be *innocent*. "You sure about that?"

"Cooper," the captain intoned, censure in that one word. "Do you know the kinds of background checks we did on her when she got a contract with us? I know you don't agree with it, but using a hypnotist to aid in witness questioning isn't some random or careless decision. We have to jump through a lot of hoops to make it legal. She's clean. Now she's in danger."

Vaughn wasn't certain he believed the first, but he knew the latter was fact.

"Ideas, gentlemen?"

"Well, she'll need protection." Bennet rubbed a hand over his jaw. "I'd say that's on us, and it'll make certain nothing dirty's going down."

"This is escalating." Captain Dean shook his head gravely. "If it goes much further, it becomes less our business and more current crime's business. We should be working with Homicide now. Cooper? What are you thinking?"

Vaughn didn't answer right away. He caught a glimpse of Ms. Torres standing next to a fireman. She had a blanket wrapped around her, and she was looking at her burned-to-ash house with tears streaming down her cheeks.

He looked away. "We've got to get her out of here." He didn't particularly like the idea that came to him, but he didn't have to like it. Bottom line, everyone else trusted this woman way too much, so if she was going to come under their protection, it needed to be *his* protection, so he could keep an eye on her.

It couldn't be anywhere near here. "My suggestion? Stevens works with Homicide, then maybe you put Griffen on it too. I take the woman up to the cabin in Guadalupe. I go over things there, keep her safe and make sure she's got nothing to do with it."

"That's gonna necessitate a lot of paperwork," Captain Dean grumbled.

"She can't stay in Austin. We've got to get her out of here. We all know it."

The captain sighed. "I'll call the necessary people. I can't argue with this being the best option. But, you know who *is* going to argue?" He pointed at Ms. Torres.

Vaughn looked at her again. She wasn't crying anymore. No, that angry expression that she'd leveled at him earlier today had taken over her face. He didn't have to be close to remember what it looked like.

Big dark eyes as shiny as the dark curls she'd pulled back from her face. The snarly curve to those sensuous lips and—

No, there was no *and*. Not when it came to this woman.

"She'll agree," Vaughn reassured the captain. He'd make sure of it.

WHEN RANGER JERK stepped next to her, Natalie didn't bother to hide her utter disgust. "Well, thanks for getting to my house after it burned down. Add that to me losing my favorite job—also your fault. Would you like to, oh, I don't know…" She wanted to say something scathing about what else he could do to ruin her life, but…

Everything she had was gone. Her house, every belonging, every memento. Worst of all, years' worth of research and information she'd gathered on Gabby's case. All gone. Everything she owned and loved gone except for her car and what she'd had in it.

She tried to breathe through a sob, but she choked on it. The tears and the emotion and the enormity of it all caught in her throat, and she had to cover her mouth with her hand to keep from crying out.

She'd been here for hours, and she couldn't wrap her head around it. She hadn't even been able to text her mom the full details because she just...

How had this happened? Why had this happened?

She sensed him move, and she hoped against hope he was walking away. That he wouldn't say a word and make this whole nightmare worse. All of this was terrible, and she didn't want Ranger Jerk rubbing it in or—worse—feeling sorry for her.

But he didn't disappear. She didn't hear retreating footsteps as tears clouded her vision. No, he moved closer. She hadn't thought much about this guy having any sort of conscience or empathy in him, but he put a big hand on her back, warm and steady.

She swallowed, wiping at the tears. It wasn't an overly familiar touch. Just his palm and fingers lightly flush with her upper back, but it was strong. It had a remarkable effect. A strange thread of calm wound through her pain.

"This is shocking and painful," he said in a low, reassuring voice. "There's no point in trying to be hard. No one should have to go through this."

She sniffled, blinking the last of the tears out of her eyes. Oh, there'd be more to come, but for now she could swallow them down, blink them back. She stared at him, trying to work through the fact he'd spoken so nicely to her. He *touched* her. "Are you comforting me?"

He grimaced. "Is that considered comfort? That's terrible comfort."

She laughed through another sob. "Oh, God, and now you're being funny." Obviously she was a little delirious, because she was starting to wonder if Ranger Jerk wasn't so terrible after all.

Then she looked back at her house. Gone. All of it *gone*. There were rangers and police and firemen and all number of official-looking people striding about, talking in low voices. Around her house. Gone. All of it gone.

Ranger Jerk could be reassuring, he could even be funny, but he couldn't deny what was in front of them. "This was on purpose," she said, her voice sounding flat and hopeless even in her own ears.

He didn't respond, but when she finally glanced at him, he nodded. His gaze was on the house too, that square jaw tensed tight enough to probably crack metal between his teeth. He made an impressive profile in the flashing lights and dark night. All angles and shadows, but there was a determination in his glare at the ruins of her house—something she'd never seen in all those other officers she'd talked to today, or eight years ago.

Confidence. Certainty. A blazing determination to right this wrong—something she recognized because it matched her own.

It bolstered her somehow. "That's why *you're* here. It's about this morning." She watched him, and finally those cool gray-blue eyes turned to her.

"Yes, that's why I'm here," he replied, his voice still low, still matter-of-fact.

Natalie had spent the past eight years learning how to deal with fear. The constancy of it, the lack of rationale behind it. But this was a new kind, and she didn't know how to suppress the shudder that went through her body.

"We're going to protect you, Ms. Torres. This is directly related to the case we brought you in on, and as long as you agree to a few things, we can keep you safe. I promise you that."

It was an odd thing to feel some ounce of comfort from those words. Because she didn't know him, and she really didn't trust him. But somehow, she did trust *that*. He was a jerk, yes, but he was a by-the-book jerk.

"What things do I need to agree to?" she asked. How much longer would her legs keep her up? She was exhausted. She'd come home after dropping her mom off at her apartment to find the neighbors in the streets and fire trucks blocking her driveway, and her house covered in either arcs of water or licks of flame.

Then, she'd been whisked behind one of the big police SUVs, made not to look at her house burning to ash in front of her, while officer after officer asked her question after question.

Oh, how she wanted to sleep. To curl up right on

the ground and wake up and find this was all some kind of nightmare.

But she'd wanted that and never got it too often to even indulge in the fantasy anymore. "Ranger J—" Oh, right, she shouldn't be calling him that out loud. "Ranger Cooper, what do I need to agree to?"

He raised an eyebrow at her misstep, but he couldn't possibly guess what she'd meant to call him just from a misplaced *j*-sound.

He pushed his hands into the pockets of his pants, looking so pressed and polished she wondered if he might be part robot.

It wasn't a particularly angry movement, sliding his hands easily into the folds of the fabric, and yet she thought the fact he would move or fidget in any way spoke to something. Something unpleasant.

"You're going to have to come with me," he finally said, his tone flat and his face expressionless.

"Go with you where?"

He let out a sigh, and she got the sinking suspicion he didn't like what was coming next any more than she was going to.

"You need to get out of Austin. There isn't time to mess around. Herman is dead. You're in *imminent* danger. You agree to come with me, the fewer questions asked the better, and trust that I will keep you safe."

"Herman is… How? When? Wh—"

"It isn't important," he said tonelessly, all that compassion she thought she'd caught a glimpse of clearly dead. "What's important is your safety."

"But I…I didn't do anything."

"You were there when Herman talked. That's enough."

She tried to process all this. "Doesn't that put you in danger too? And Ranger Stevens?"

He shrugged. "That's part and parcel with the job. We're trained to deal with danger. You, ma'am, are not."

She wanted to bristle at that. Oh, she knew plenty about danger, but no, she wasn't a ranger, or even a police officer. She didn't carry a weapon, and as much as she'd lived with all the possibilities of the horrors of human nature haunting her for eight years, she didn't know how to fight it.

She only knew how to dissect it. How to want to find the truth in it. She needed…help. She needed to take it if only because losing her would likely kill her grandmother and mother like losing Gabby had likely killed Dad.

Natalie swallowed at the panic in her throat. "My family? Are they safe? It's only my mother and my grandmother, but…"

"We'll talk with different agencies to keep them protected, as well. For the time being, it doesn't look like they'd be in any danger, but we'll keep our eye on the situation."

She nodded, trying to breathe. Mom would hate

that, just as she hated all police. She'd hate it as much as she hated Natalie working for the Texas Rangers, but Natalie couldn't quite agree with Mom's hate.

Oh, she'd hated any and all law enforcement for a while, but she'd tirelessly tried to find her own answers, and she knew how frustrating it could be. She also knew men like Ranger Cooper, as off-putting and as much of a jerk as he was, took their jobs seriously. They tried, and when they failed, it affected them.

She'd seen sorrow and guilt in too many officers' eyes to count.

"I'll go with you," she said, her voice a ragged, abused thing.

His eyes widened, and he turned fully to her. "You will?" He didn't bother to hide his surprise.

She was a little surprised herself, but it would get her the thing she wanted more than anything else in the world. Information. "I will come with you and follow whatever your office suggests in order to keep me safe. On one condition."

The surprise easily morphed into his normal scowl of disdain. "You're being protected, Ms. Torres. You don't get to have conditions."

"I want to know about the case. I want to know what I'm running from."

"That's confidential."

"You're taking me 'away from Austin' to protect me. I don't even know you."

He gave her a once-over, and she at once knew he

didn't trust her. While she was sure he was the kind of man who would protect her anyway, his distrust grated. So, she held her ground, emotionally wrung out and exhausted. She stood there and accepted his distrustful perusal.

"I'll see what information I'm allowed to divulge to you, but you're going to have to come down to the office right now to get everything squared away. We'll be leaving the minute we have it all figured out with legal."

"Will we?"

"You don't have to do it my way, Ms. Torres, but I can guarantee you no one's way is better than mine."

She wouldn't take that guarantee for a million dollars, but she'd take a chance. A chance for information. If she was going to lose everything, she was darn well going to get closer to finding Gabby out of it.

"All right, Ranger Cooper. We'll do it your way." For now.

Chapter Three

Vaughn was exhausted, but he swallowed the yawn and focused on the long, winding road ahead of him.

Natalie dozed in the passenger seat, making only the random soft sleeping noise. Vaughn didn't look—not once—he focused.

The midday sun reflected against the road, creating the illusion of a sparkling ribbon of moving water. They still had another three hours to go to get to the mountains and his little cabin. Which meant he'd spent the past *four* hours talking himself out of all his second thoughts.

It was the only way to keep *her* safe and *him* certain she was innocent. She'd agreed to everything without so much as a peep. He didn't know if he distrusted that or if she was just too devastated and exhausted to mount any kind of argument.

She stirred, and he checked his rearview mirror again. The white sedan was still following them. There was enough space between their cars; he'd thought he was simply being paranoid for noticing.

That had been two hours ago. Two hours of that car following him at the same exact distance.

He cursed.

"What?" Natalie mumbled, straightening in the seat. "You're not going to run out of gas, are you?" She rubbed her eyes, back arching as she stretched and moved her neck from side to side.

With more force than he cared to admit, he looked away from her and directly at the road. "No. Listen to me. Do not look back. Do not move. We're being tailed."

"What?"

She started to whip her head toward the back—obnoxious woman—but he reached over with one hand and squeezed her thigh.

She screeched and slapped his hand. "Don't touch me."

He removed his hand, gripped the wheel with both now. Tried to erase any…reaction from touching her like that. It had only been a diversionary tactic. "Then do as you're told and don't look back."

Her shoulders went rigid and she stared straight ahead, eyes wide, breathing uneven. "You really think…"

"I could be wrong. I'd rather be safe and wrong than wrong and sorry." He looked at the mile marker, tried to focus on what was around them, where they could lose the tail. What it would mean if they couldn't.

Natalie grasped her knees, obviously panicking.

As much as he knew he could figure this out, he understood that she was lost. Fire burning all of her possessions and sleepless nights on the road with a near stranger weren't exactly calming events.

"It'll be fine," he said, mustering all of his compassion—what little of that was left. "I've dodged better tails than this."

"Have you?"

"Do you know a Texas Ranger has to have eight years of police work with a major crimes division before they're even qualified to apply?"

Natalie huffed out an obviously unimpressed breath. "So you had to write speeding tickets for eight years? Didn't mean you had to dodge people following you."

Vaughn didn't bother responding. Speeding tickets? Not for a long, long time. But he wasn't going to tell her about the undercover operations he'd worked, the homicides he'd solved. He wasn't going to waste precious brain space proving to her that he was the best man to keep her safe.

Maybe when they got to the cabin he could just give her Jenny's number and his ex-wife could fill Ms. Torres in on all the ways he'd put himself in danger during his years as a police officer.

Frustrated with *that* line of thought, he jerked the wheel to get off the highway and onto an out-of-the-way exit at the last second.

Unfortunately, the white sedan did the same.

"We're going to stop at the first gas station we find. We're both going to get out, go inside and pretend to look for snacks. I'm going to talk to the attendant. You will stand in the candy aisle and wait for my sign."

"What's your sign?" she said after a gulp.

"You'll know it when you see it."

"But..."

"No buts. We have to play some things by ear." Like what the purpose of an hours-long tail was. If it was to take them out, Vaughn had to believe they would have already attempted something. The hanging back and just following pointed more to an information-grabbing tail.

It took a few miles, but a little town with a gas station finally appeared on the horizon. Vaughn kept his speed steady as he drove toward it, worked to keep himself calm as he pulled into a parking spot.

"We get out. We act normal. You watch me, and you follow absolutely any and all orders I give you. Got it?"

Natalie blinked at the gas station in front of them, and he could tell she wanted to argue, but the woman apparently had *some* sense because she finally nodded.

Vaughn got out of the car first, and Natalie followed. She didn't exactly look *calm*, but she didn't bolt or run. She met him at the front of the car.

Vaughn didn't like it, but they had to look at least

a little casual. Maybe these guys knew exactly who they were, but playing a part gave him a better shot of putting doubts in their heads.

So, he linked fingers with Ms. Torres and walked like any two involved people might into the building. Her hand was clammy, and he gave it a little reassuring squeeze. He leaned close to her ear, hoping the two men outside were paying attention to the intimate move.

"Go along with anything I do or say," he said, low enough so that the cashier couldn't hear.

She didn't say anything or nod, but she didn't argue with him, either. In fact, she held tightly on to his hand.

When he took a deep breath, all he could smell was the smoke that must still be in her hair from early this morning, but underneath there was some hint of something sweet.

Lack of sleep was making him delirious. "Go find a snack, honey," he said, doing his best to infect some ease into his exaggerated drawl. With only a little wobble, she let go of his hand and walked toward the candy aisle.

Casually Vaughn sauntered to the counter. He glanced at the scratch-off tickets displayed, then glanced out the doors where the white sedan was parked, one of the men filling it up.

Vaughn flicked his glance to the bored-looking cashier. "Ma'am," he said with a nod. He slid his badge across the counter to where the cashier could see it. She didn't flinch or even act impressed or moved. She popped her gum at him.

He wouldn't be deterred. "I need you to call the local police department. I need you to give them the following license plate number, description and my DSN."

She didn't make a move to get a pen or paper. Vaughn glanced out of the corner of his eye to where the white sedan and two men in big coats and big hats stood. One eyeing his truck, the other eyeing the store and Natalie.

Vaughn flicked his jacket out of the way so the cashier could also see his gun. "This is official police business. Call the local police department and give them the following information." He inclined his head to the pen that was settled on top of the cash register keyboard. "Now."

The woman swallowed this time, and she grabbed the pen.

Vaughn looked back at Natalie who was shaking in the candy aisle. He rattled off the information to the cashier.

He kept tabs on the men outside who were obviously keeping tabs on him. "Make the call now. Whatever you do, don't tell those men out there. Got it?"

The now-nervous cashier gave a little nod and picked up the phone on the counter next to the cash register.

As he moved away from the counter, one of the

men started walking toward the door. Still, Vaughn didn't panic. He'd been in a lot stickier situations than this, no matter what Ms. Hypnotist thought of his past experience.

He approached Natalie, watching to make sure the cashier got the information to the local police before the man entered the door.

It was a close call, but the cashier had some survival instincts herself and she hung up just as the man walked inside.

Vaughn took Natalie's arm. "Let's go to the bathroom."

She arched a brow, all holier-than-thou, even though terror was clearly lurking in the depths of those big dark eyes. "Together?"

"Yes, ma'am." He nodded toward the back of the store where the bathroom sign was. "Move. And whatever you do, don't look behind us."

She started to walk toward the bathroom, still shaking, still braving it out. He'd give her credit for that.

Later.

"You know, every time you tell me not to do something, I only want to do it more?"

"Okay, don't look straight ahead. Don't step into the women's bathroom, and certainly don't let me follow you inside."

Surprisingly, she did exactly what he wanted her to do.

NATALIE COULDN'T STOP SHAKING. She knew it showed weakness, and she tried to be stronger than that. For Gabby. For the hope that Gabby was still alive to be found.

But, she was so scared she wanted to cry. Someone was following them. Ranger Cooper seemed more than capable, but that didn't make it any less scary. It didn't erase her house being gone, and it most certainly didn't erase the fact someone was apparently *following* them.

Ranger Cooper immediately locked the door behind them as they stepped into the women's restroom. He was a blur, moving about the small room and the even smaller stalls, and she had no idea what he was looking for.

So, she simply stood in the center trying to find her own center. Trying to focus on what she was doing this for. On who she was doing this for. She'd pursued details of Gabby's case with a dogged tenacity that had alienated every friend, significant other and her own grandmother. Even Mom was close to losing any and all patience with her.

But how could they give up? How could *she* give up? Maybe she'd never anticipated this kind of danger, but that didn't mean she was going to shake apart and hide away. Gabby was somewhere out there.

She had to be. *He keeps the girls.* Maybe it wasn't Gabby's case, but maybe it *was.* She needed information, which meant she needed Ranger Cooper.

After a full sweep of the bathroom, he pulled his phone out of his pocket and typed something into it. Natalie simply watched him because she didn't know what else to do. She counted each time his blunt, long finger touched the screen to keep herself from panicking.

When he glanced up from his phone, those steely blue eyes meeting hers with a blank kind of certainty, she thought she might panic anyway.

"We can't waste much more time," he said, his voice as low and gravelly as she'd ever heard it. Surely he was exhausted. Even Texas Rangers got tired. Even Texas Rangers were human and mortal.

She'd really prefer to think of him as superhuman, and he made it almost seem possible when he flipped back his coat and pulled the weapon at his hip from its holster.

"If it gets back to whoever sent them they're being detained, we'll just get another tail."

Natalie subdued the shaking, jittering fear in her limbs and focused on what had gotten her here. Questions. Information. "But how can we get past them? Won't they just report back to… Do you know who it is? Is this about The Stallion? I couldn't find any information on what exactly that is. A man? A gang?"

Ranger Cooper took a menacing step toward her, reminding her of that moment in the interrogation room when he'd stepped between her and Mr. Herman.

Dead Mr. Herman.

She closed her eyes and tried to focus on how much she'd hated him then. Hated him for getting in her way.

"Do not ask questions, Ms. Torres. The less you know, the better. For your own good. Now…" He curled those long fingers around the grips of his gun. "Listen to me carefully. Do everything I say to the letter. For your own good. Let me repeat that," he said, as if talking to a small child.

"For your own good, you will do as I say. Stay behind me. Listen to me and only me. Whatever you do, don't make a sound. If we can get a little bit of a head start, we're golden. Got it?"

She couldn't speak. Every muscle in her body was seized too tightly to allow her to speak, or nod.

"Torres." It was whispered, but it was a harsh bark. "Got it?"

She managed a squeaky yes, and as he unlocked the door, she stayed behind him. As much as she didn't like him, in this moment, she would have pressed herself to his back if he'd asked her to.

He might be a jerk, but he seemed to know what he was doing. Right now, with two bulky men speaking to two decidedly not bulky local police officers in front of the cash register, she pretty much *had* to trust Ranger Cooper would get them out of this.

She met gazes with one of the bulky men, and though he had his hat low on his head, she could feel the cold, black gaze.

"Behind me, Torres," Ranger Cooper whispered with enough authority to have her feet moving faster.

One of the bulky men tried to sidestep one of the local officers, but the local officer didn't back off.

"Move again, sir, and I will pull my weapon on you."

"We ain't done anything wrong, boy."

Ranger Cooper grabbed her arm. "Move," he instructed, and she realized belatedly she'd all but stopped. But she was being propelled out the door, a skirmish breaking out behind them. "Get in the car. Now. Fast."

On shaky legs, she did as she was told, but managed to glance back in time to see Ranger Cooper shoving a broom through the handles of the door. Which caused the men inside to push against the police officers even harder, even getting past one to get to the door.

Natalie got into the truck's passenger seat, her breath coming in little puffs. That broom handle wouldn't hold them in for very long. If only because there had to be another exit, and it already looked as though the officers inside were losing the battle.

But Ranger Cooper wasn't getting in the truck. She tried to breathe deeply, but a little whimpering sound came out instead.

"Get it together. Get it together," she whispered to herself, craning her neck to see where Ranger Cooper had gone.

She watched as he casually walked over to a white sedan, weapon held to his side where only someone really paying attention could see. Then he held the muzzle of the gun to the front tire and pulled the trigger.

Even knowing it was coming, Natalie jumped when the shot rang out. Ranger Cooper was back in the truck in the blink of an eye, and Natalie glanced at the store where the two men had disappeared from the windowed doors. No doubt looking for another exit.

"That'll buy us some time," Ranger Cooper muttered, zooming out of the parking lot without so much as buckling his seat belt.

"What about those police officers? The cashier?"

He merely nodded into the distance. "Hear that?"

She didn't at first, but after a few seconds she could make out sirens.

"Backup," he said, his eyes focused on the road, his hands tight on the wheel. "Since the guys fought back, they can arrest them. But that doesn't mean there aren't more tails on us. We have to be vigilant. I want you to keep your eyes peeled. Anything seems suspicious, you mention it. I don't care how silly it sounds. We can't be too careful now."

Natalie gripped the handle of the door with one hand, pressed the other, in a fist, to her stomach.

She was in so far over her head she almost laughed. She knew Ranger Cooper wouldn't appreciate that, and she was a little afraid if she started laughing, it'd turn into crying soon enough.

She was too tough for that. Too determined. No more crying. No more shaking. No more panic. If they had bad guys to face down, she was at least going to pull her weight.

Because if she did, if they could get through all this, Gabby might be on the other side. Everything she'd been working for over the past eight years.

Yeah, no more panic. She had a sister to save.

Chapter Four

Vaughn didn't know if he trusted how relatively easy it had been to fool the tail. Or the fact another hadn't taken its place. All in all, he didn't understand what that tail had been trying to accomplish, and without knowing...

Frustrated, he scanned the road again. The Guadalupe Mountains loomed in the distance of an arid landscape. The hardscrabble desert stretched out for miles, the craggy, spindly peaks of the Guadalupes offering the only respite to endless flat.

The cabin was still forty-five minutes away, and they were the only car on this old desert highway. If he had a tail, it was a much better one.

He flicked a glance at Torres. Thinking about her as a last name helped things. He could think of her as a partner, as just a *person* he had to work with. Not a complicated mystery of a woman.

The only problem was, he didn't trust her as far as he could throw her, and that was the key to any partnership.

She sat in the passenger seat, her eyes still too

big, her hands still clenched too tight. Her olive skin tone had paled considerably, but she'd gotten control of her shaking.

"You did good," he found himself saying, out of nowhere. She *had* done good for a civilian, but he had no idea why he was praising her. What the hell was the point of that?

"I just did what you told me to do."

"Exactly."

She rolled her eyes and shook her head. "You really are a piece of work, Ranger Cooper."

"Not everyone could have gotten through that, Ms. Torres. Some people freeze, some people cry, some people…" Why was he explaining this to her? If she didn't want to believe she'd done a good thing, what did he care? But his mouth just kept *going*. "There's a lot of pressure when you're under a threat, and the smartest thing you can do is listen to the person who has the coolest head. You did that. You made good choices and had good instincts."

"Well, thank you." She blew out a breath, and he noted that the hands she'd had in fists loosened incrementally.

"I wish I didn't know just *how* much I can stand up in the face of a threat," she muttered.

"Unfortunately, that was only the beginning."

"You're a constant comfort, Ranger Cooper."

She fell silent for a few moments, and he thought maybe they could make it all the way to the cabin without having any more of the discussion, certainly not any more of him telling her she'd done well. But she began to fidget. The kind of fidgeting that would lead to questioning.

It appeared that whatever nerves or fear that had kept Ms. Torres from interrogating him about what was going on had been eradicated or managed.

"Who's after us? And why? What do I have to do with any of this?" she asked, thankfully sounding more exasperated than scared.

Scared tended to pull at that do-gooder center of him. He tried to focus on *cases* rather than people. But he could get irritated with exasperation. Why couldn't she just trust him to keep her safe and leave it at that?

But he knew that she wouldn't, and he had been given permission to share certain details with her.

Considering he still didn't trust this woman, he wasn't about to give her really important details.

He focused on the road, the flat, unending desert ahead of him. "You were in the interrogation room when Herman talked."

"He didn't even say anything that was any kind of incrimination. Certainly nothing that I would understand to be able to tell anyone. And I *ruined* your interrogation. They should be sending me flowers, not…fire."

The corner of his lip twitched as if…as if he wanted to smile. Which was very…strange. But the fact she owned up to ruining the interrogation, while also making a little bit of a joke in what had to be a very scary situation for her, he appreciated that. He almost admired it. God knew he didn't make light of much of anything.

"In all likelihood, they don't know what exactly was said," Vaughn told her. *Nothing* about his tone was self-deprecating or light, which he never would have noticed if not for her. "All it took was the knowledge that he was interrogated, and that we started looking into the name he mentioned. When you're mixed up in organized crime, that's enough to get you killed."

She pressed her lips together as if a wave of emotion had swept over her. Her eyes even looked a little shiny. When she spoke, there was a slight tremor to her voice. "I just keep thinking about how he said he had a daughter, and his wife had cancer, and he's just…dead."

"He worked for a man who has likely killed more people than we'll ever know about. Herman knew what he was getting himself into and the risks he was taking. Even if he wasn't the muscle, and even if he had a family, he made bad choices that he knew very well had chances of getting him killed."

"So you're saying he deserved to die?" Natalie asked in that same tremulous voice.

It had been a long time since someone had made him feel bad about the callousness he had to employ, *had* to build to endure a career in law enforcement, and especially unsolved crimes. He didn't care for the way she did it so easily. Just a question and a tremor.

But this was *reality*, and clearly Torres didn't have a clue about that. "It's not my place to determine whether he deserved anything. I'm putting forth the reality of the situation."

"I don't understand why they burned down my house, why they *killed* a man, just because he mentioned a name and you started asking questions. How is that worth following us across Texas? I mean, if they were going to kill us, wouldn't they have already done it?"

"Yes."

She waited, and he could feel her gaze on him, but he didn't have anything else to say to that.

"Yes? That's it? You're just going to agree with me, and that's it?"

"Well, honestly, they probably did try to kill you with that fire. You were lucky you weren't home. What more of an explanation would you like?"

"One that makes sense!"

He could tell by the way she quieted after her little outburst that she hadn't meant to let that emotion show. Especially when the next words she spoke were lower, calmer.

"I want to know why this is happening. I want to understand why I'm in more danger than you or Ranger Stevens. Why my house was burned down, not yours."

"I can't speculate on why they burned your house down. The reason that Stevens and I aren't in as much danger is because we're police officers. We're trained to look for danger, and quite frankly going after us is a lot worse for them than going after you. Anyone hurts a member of law enforcement, the police aren't going to rest until they find him."

"But if you go after a civilian, it's fine?" she demanded incredulously.

She gave him *such* a headache. He took a deep breath, because he wasn't going to snap at her for deliberately misinterpreting his words. He wasn't going to yell at her for not getting it. She wasn't an officer; she couldn't understand.

"We're family, Ms. Torres," he said evenly and calmly, never taking his eyes off the road. "It's like if a stranger is gunned down in the street or your sister is gunned down in the street, which one are you going to avenge a little bit harder?"

Something in what he'd said seemed to impact her a little more than it should have. She paled further and looked down at her lap. He wasn't sure if she was more scared now, or if she was upset by something.

"I'm going to keep you safe, Ms. Torres," he assured her, because as much as he avoided those soft, comforting feelings almost all of the time, that was his duty. He would do it, no matter what.

"Why?" she asked in a small voice. "I'm not law

enforcement. I'm not your family. Why should I feel like you're going to keep me safe?"

"Because you came under my protection, and I don't take that lightly."

"I can't understand what they think I can do," she said, her voice going quieter with each sentence, her face turning toward the window as if she wanted to hide from him.

He was fine with that. He'd be even finer if he could stop answering her questions. "The thing about crime and criminals is that they don't often follow rational trains of thought like we do. Their motivations and morals are skewed."

"That almost sounds philosophical, Ranger Cooper."

"It's just the truth. It's easier to accept the truth and figure out what you can do about it than to wish it was different or understandable."

"But…what am I supposed to do? How am I supposed to… I have other jobs, and a family, and… It's all hitting me how much I'm los—"

"You're saving your life. Period. You won't have a job or a family to go back to if you're dead."

"Again, such a comfort."

"At this point, it's more important that we are honest than it is that I comfort you. Right now you're safe because you're with me. That's the only reason. I need you to not forget that."

"I don't expect you to allow me to forget it," she

returned, reminding him of that hallway when she'd blamed him for getting her removed from the Rangers. Though it was frustrating that it was geared at *him,* her anger would serve them well. It would keep her moving, it would keep her brave.

"It's best if you don't. For the both of us. You're not the only one in danger here, you're just the only one who doesn't know what to do about it."

"What about Ranger Stevens?"

"Ranger Stevens can keep himself out of danger. All I need you to do is worry about listening to me. If you do that, everything will be fine."

"How do you know?"

"Because I give everything to my job. There is nothing about what I do that I take lightly."

So everyone had always told him. Too serious. Too dedicated. Too wrapped up in a career that didn't give him time for much of anything else.

But people didn't understand that it gave him everything. A sense of usefulness, a sense of order in a chaotic world. It gave him the ability to face any challenge that was laid before him.

Maybe it gives you a way to keep everyone at a safe distance. It irritated him that those words came into his head, even more irritating that they were in his ex-wife's voice. He hadn't thought about Jenny in over a year. Why had the past two days brought back some of that old bitterness?

But he didn't have time to figure it out. He had to get to the cabin, and he had to solve this case.

Personal problems always came after the job, and if the job never ended… Well, so be it.

No MATTER HOW exhausted she was, all Natalie could do was watch as the desert gave way to mountain. They began to drive up…and up. There were signs for Guadalupe Mountains National Park, but they didn't drive into it. Instead, Ranger Cooper took winding roads that seemed to weave around the mountains and the park markers.

There weren't houses or other cars on the road. There was nothing. Nothing except rock and the low-lying green brush that was only broken up by the random cactus.

He turned onto a very bumpy dirt road that curved and twisted up a rolling swell of land covered in green brush. After she didn't know how long, a building finally came into view.

Nestled into that sloping green swell of land, with the impressive almost square jut of the mountains behind it, was a little postage stamp of a cabin made almost entirely of stone. It looked ancient, almost part of the landscape.

And it was very, very small. She was going to stay here in this isolated, tiny cabin with this man who rubbed her all kinds of the wrong way.

"What is this place?" she asked, the nerves making her almost as shaky as she'd been earlier.

"It's my private family cabin."

"You have a family?" She couldn't picture him with loved ones, a wife and kids. It bothered her on some odd level.

He slid her a glance as he pulled the truck around to the back of the cabin and parked. "I did come from a mother and a father, not just sprung from the ground fully made."

"The second scenario seems much more plausible," she retorted, realizing too late that she needed to rein in all her snark.

She thought for one tiny glimmer of a second his mouth might have curved into some approximation of a smile.

Apparently she was becoming delusional. *But he doesn't have a wife or kids.* Really, really delusional.

"My sister stays here quite frequently as well, so hopefully you should be able to find some things of hers you can use."

"Oh, I wouldn't feel right about—"

"You don't have a choice, Ms. Torres. You don't have *anything*. And before you repeat it for a third time, yes, I realize I am of literally no comfort to you."

"Well, at least I don't have to say it for a third time."

He let out a hefty sigh and then got out of his truck.

She followed suit, stepping into the warm afternoon sun. The air had a certain...she couldn't put her finger on a word for it. It didn't feel as heavy as the air in Austin. There was a clarity to it. A purity. She couldn't see another living soul, possibly another living thing. All that existed around her was this vast, arid landscape.

And a very unfortunately sexy Texas Ranger who appeared to be exploring the perimeter of his family cabin.

Even after being up since whatever time he had got up to go to her burned-out house, after all the time getting everything squared away to secret her out of Austin, after the incident at the gas station and driving across Texas, he was unwrinkled and fresh. All she felt was dirty and grimy and disgusting. She *smelled*, and she was afraid to even glance at what the desert air had done to her hair.

She stood next to the truck, waiting for her orders. Because God knew Ranger Cooper would have orders for her.

He disappeared around the corner of the cabin, and Natalie leaned against the truck and looked up at the hazy blue sky. She let the sun soak into her skin.

For the first time since before the fire, she had a moment to breathe and really think. All of this open space made her think about Gabby. How long she'd been gone, where she was... Did she still get to see things like this?

Natalie tried to fight the thoughts and tears, but she was exhausted. They trickled over her eyelashes and down her cheeks. She tried to wipe them away, but they kept falling.

She'd worked relentlessly and tirelessly for eight years to try to find Gabby, and she thought she'd been close. A hint. *He keeps the girls.* But now she was far away from Austin, and she was with this man who couldn't pull a punch to save his life.

The hope she had doggedly held on to for eight years was seriously and utterly shaken.

What could she do here? What could she do when her whole life right now was just staying alive? People were after her, and she didn't even know why.

Why was she crying now, though? She was finally safe. She knew Ranger Cooper would do his duty. He didn't seem like the type of man who could do anything but.

Why was it now that she felt like she was falling apart?

"Everything looks good out here. I'm going to check the inside, but I need you to follow me."

No please, no warmth, just an order. She kept her face turned to the sky, trying to wipe away all traces of the tears before she faced him. She took a deep breath and let it out.

She'd had a little breakdown, and now it was over. She'd let some air out of the pressure in her chest, and now she could move forward. She just needed a goal.

She glanced at Ranger Cooper, who was standing at the door, all stiff, gruff policeman.

She needed more information. That was the goal. Information was the goal. She couldn't lose sight of that even though he was so bad at giving it.

She began to walk toward him, wondering what made anyone in his family think this was a good place for a little getaway cabin. It was rocky and sharp and dry. If you looked closely at all, everything seemed so ugly.

But when you looked away from the ground, and took in the home and the full extent of the landscape, there was something truly awe inspiring about it. It was big and vast, this world they lived in. She never had that feeling in the middle of Austin.

She walked over to the porch. It was hard to follow orders and listen to what someone else told her to do. She wasn't used to that. She had been such a strong force in her life for the past few years. She had made all the choices, asked all the questions, sought all the answers. She'd even alienated her grandmother in her quest to find Gabby, so sitting back and doing what someone else told her to do was…hard. It went against everything she had put her whole life into.

But she knew that knee-jerk reaction didn't have a place here. Not when she was with a Texas Ranger who obviously knew way more than she did about safety and criminals.

She was going to have to bury the instinct to argue

with him, and it was going to be as big of a challenge as trusting him would be.

"The chances of anyone having breached the cabin are extremely low," he said, opening the door and analyzing the frame as though it might grow weapons and attack them. "But when you're dealing with criminals of this magnitude, you can't be too careful. Which means I can't leave you outside. I can't let you out of my sight. So, I'm going to go inside and make sure there's nothing off. I need you to follow right behind me, carefully mirroring my every step. Can you do that?"

"Can I walk behind you and do what you do?"

"Yes, that is the question."

She gritted her teeth. He didn't think she could walk? He didn't think she could do anything, did he? He thought she was some flighty, foolish *hypnotist* who couldn't follow easy orders.

Arrogant jerk of a man. "Yes, I can do that," she said through those gritted teeth.

"Excellent. Let's go."

He stepped over the threshold, immediately turning toward the left. She followed him, and since her job was to follow exactly in his footsteps, she watched him. That ease of movement he had about him, the surety in the way he strode into the cabin looking for whatever he was looking for.

He was all packed muscle, but there was something like grace in his movements. It was mesmerizing, and she had no problem following him around the inside of the stone cabin.

They did an entire tour of the kitchen and living area, which were both open, and then down a very narrow hallway that led to two bedrooms and a bathroom. All the rooms were small, and the stone that composed the outside of the cabin were used for the inside walls and floor as well.

It wasn't cozy exactly. It was beautiful, but it wasn't the sort of log mountain cabin she had in her head. There weren't warm colorful blankets or cute artwork on the walls. It was all very gray and minimalist.

"You have something against color?" she asked, forgetting to keep her thoughts to herself.

He glanced over his shoulder at her, and the question was kind of funny in light of the way his blue eyes looked even grayer here. It was like even the color of his body didn't dare shine in this space.

"If you're looking for color…" He opened the door to the last bedroom and stepped inside, doing his little police thing where he looked at every corner and around every lamp and out every window.

But Natalie didn't follow him this time. Where the rest of the cabin was stone and stark and sort of reflective of the outside landscape, this room was a riot and explosion of color. It was glitter and fringe.

"What on earth is all this?"

"This is my sister's room. Which means that, right

now, it is your room, and you can feel free to use any-thing that's in here." He opened the closet and rifled through it. She still had no idea what exactly he was looking for, but she knew if she asked he would only give her some irritating half answer.

"I feel really strange about using your sister's things."

"Trust me, my sister has nothing but things, and when I explain to her why someone used them, she will be more than fine with it. As I reminded you ear-lier, you don't have a choice."

"Because I have nothing. Yes, let's keep talking about that."

He gave her a cursory once-over, just like he'd given the cabin. She wouldn't be surprised if he checked her pulse and teeth or frisked her for a wire.

She tried not to think too hard about the little shiver that ran through her at the thought of his hands on her. Those big hands that had covered so much space on her back when he'd placed them there in comfort after her house had been decimated.

She swallowed and looked away.

"Sleep." He barked the order, then walked right past her without a second glance or word. The door closed with a soft click, and she could only gape at the rough-hewn wood.

He was ordering her to *sleep*? The absolute gall of the man. How dare he tell her what she needed? She had half a mind to march right out of the room and tell him she was *fine*.

But, God, she was tired. So, for today, he'd get his way. *And probably for tomorrow and the next day and the next, because he is in charge here, remember?*

She sighed at that depressing thought and crawled into bed, hopeful to sleep all the tears away.

Chapter Five

Vaughn stared at his laptop screen and tried not to doze off. He would need to wake up Torres soon, if only so he could sleep. The tail had left him jumpy, and he didn't want both of them asleep at the same time at any point.

Unfortunately he was tired enough that the words of his files were simply jumbled letters. It was beyond frustrating he couldn't concentrate. Had he gone soft? He hadn't had a stakeout or any sort of challenging hard-on-the-body thing in a while. Had he lost his touch?

He scrubbed his hands over his face. This was ridiculous. He was fine. There was only so much the human body could handle and still be expected to concentrate on complex facts. Complex facts that had been hard enough to work out when he was well rested and well fed.

At the thought of food, his stomach grumbled. If he couldn't sleep, then he could at least eat. If he made something, then Natalie could eat when she woke up.

There wouldn't be anything fresh in the pantry, but they always kept a few extras on hand just in case. The nearest store was over an hour away, and while that was pretty damn inconvenient a lot of the time, between Vaughn's desire for complete off-the-grid privacy when he wasn't working and his sister's need for a secret spot, it worked.

He and Lucy had handled their father's fame in completely opposite ways. Lucy had embraced it. She'd followed it, becoming almost as famous a country singer as their father had been. She used the cabin only when she needed a quick, quiet, away-from-publicity break, which was rare.

Vaughn had hated the spotlight. Always. Like his mother, he hadn't been able to stand the fishbowl existence.

So he'd found a way to have almost no recognition whatsoever. He'd gotten a strange enjoyment out of going undercover back in the day, knowing no one knew who he was related to.

"You are one screwy piece of work, Cooper," he muttered, grabbing two cans of soup out of the pantry and digging up the can opener.

"Do you always talk to yourself?"

His hand flew to the butt of his weapon before he even thought about it. Before he recognized the voice, before he had a chance to smooth out the movement so Natalie wouldn't know what he had meant to do.

Quickly he put his hands back to work opening the

soup, and he purposefully didn't look at her because he didn't want to see that familiar look on her face. Jenny would cry for days after he had moments like that one, wondering why he couldn't ever shut it off, that natural reaction.

Why the hell couldn't he keep his mind off his past? Dad, Jenny. Why was it in his head, mucking things up when he had to be completely clearheaded and one hundred percent in the game right now?

"I'm heating some soup if you'd like some," he offered, ignoring her previous question.

"Have you been awake this whole time?"

"Someone needs to remain vigilant."

"You can't stay awake forever."

"No, I can't. Which means at some point, I'll have to trust you enough to take over the lookout position."

He finally happened to glance at her, and she had her lips pressed together in a disapproving line. As though she was surprised to hear that he didn't trust her. He'd been nothing but clear on that front. She shouldn't be surprised.

"The only option for beverage is water, and you're going to have to learn to live on the nonperishable staples in the pantry. I don't think it's safe to go to town, and certainly not worth it unless we absolutely have to."

She finally walked from the little opening of the hallway toward the table that acted as the eating area.

She had visible bags under her dark eyes, and her

hair was a tangled, curly mass. The smell of smoke drifted toward him even when they were yards apart.

"The soup will keep if you want to take a shower."

"I don't suppose there's a washer and dryer around here, is there?"

"Actually, there is in the hall closet. As isolated as this cabin is, my sister isn't one to do without the modern conveniences of life. We've got a good generator and plenty of appliances."

She glanced at him then, some unreadable expression on her face. She scratched a fingernail across the corner of the old wooden table that had belonged to his grandparents decades ago. Lucy might be all up in the modern conveniences, but she had a sentimental streak that ran much deeper than his.

"Are you close with your sister?"

There was something in the way that she asked the question… Something that gave him the feeling he got when things on a case weren't fitting together the way he thought they should.

There was something this woman was hiding. Even if she had nothing to do with The Stallion or Herman, there was something going on here. He needed to figure it out.

"Well, our careers make it pretty hard for us to spend time together, but we like each other well enough. Do you have a sister?"

Her downturned gaze flicked to his and then

quickly back to the table again. There was something there. Definitely.

"We were very close growing up. But…"

"But what?"

"She's…" Natalie swallowed. "Gone."

And he was an ass. Her sister had died, and he was suspicious of this woman, who probably still had painful feelings over it. "I'm sorry," he offered, surprised at how genuine it sounded coming out of him.

She glanced at him again, this time those dark eyes stayed on his a little longer. That full mouth nearly curved. "Thank you," she said. "You know, not many people just say I'm sorry. They always have to add on and make it worse."

"It may shock you to know that I'm not much of a 'add more to it' kinda guy."

This time, she didn't just smile, she laughed. The smile did something to her face, seemed to lighten that heavy sadness that had waved off her. She was pretty; it couldn't be ignored.

She's more than pretty.

But that would *have* to be ignored. He had no business thinking of her as anything other than a civilian under his protection. He shouldn't notice that she was pretty, or the curve of her hips, or the way her smile changed the light in her eyes. He shouldn't and couldn't notice these things. Not and do what he needed to do.

"So, Ranger Cooper, tell me about your cooking skills," she said, moving toward the kitchen.

"Well, first let's not set any expectations here. I have reheating skills, and that's about it. Lucky for you, there is no chance of doing anything other than reheating for the next couple days."

"Well, whatever it is, it smells delicious. I'm starving. But I do want to take a shower."

"Everything should be in the bathroom. If you don't find it in the shower, there should be a container under the sink with things like soap. As for towels, I packed a few. I'll grab you one from my bag."

She nodded without a word, and he left the soup on low heat so he could fetch her towel.

It was strange to have another presence in the cabin with him. He only ever came here alone, unless it was Christmas, and then sometimes he and Lucy would come up here with Mom.

He'd always felt like there was plenty of room when they were here. It was a small place, but Lucy had her room and he had his. If Mom came, he never minded sleeping on the couch.

Ms. Torres seemed to take up a lot of space.

Something about the way she moved, the way she smelled underneath that smoke. There was… Something there. He couldn't put a finger on it.

Perhaps that was the thing that made her feel like such a larger presence. Because he couldn't get a handle on her, he couldn't figure out what made her tick.

But he would.

He strode into his room and grabbed the duffel bag he had packed in haste. He jerked the zipper and then stopped as she stepped into the room with him.

He had meant for her to wait in the living room, or at least out in the hall, but here she was—in his space. There was something about it that set him on edge. There was something about *her* that set him on edge.

"How come the only color is in your sister's room?"

"I don't know," he returned with a grunt.

"You seem like the kind of guy who knows everything."

"I know important things. However, I don't give a damn about interior design."

She leaned against the door frame. "Well, it's a lovely place."

"It's something."

"Do you ever get lonely out here?"

The last thing he needed to think about right now was how lonely he was and for how long. He jerked the first towel his hand touched out of the bag and tossed it at her. She caught it, albeit clumsily.

She cocked her head at him. She seemed to be forever doing that, and he couldn't help but wonder if this was some sort of hypnotist trick. Cock her head, look as though she knew exactly what was going on in his mind even though there was no way that she possibly could.

"Thanks. I'll go take a shower, and then you can get some sleep. That is, if you trust me enough?"

She said it sarcastically, because she probably knew he didn't have a choice. At this point, if he didn't purposefully and decisively take a nap, he was going to keel over and fall asleep against his will. "Trust is a two-way street, Ms. Torres."

"Natalie. Please call me Natalie. I am so tired of hearing you drawl *Ms.* in that condescending Texas Ranger tone."

"Fine. Natalie." Something about saying her full name aloud with her big dark eyes on him shimmered through him. He was tired of this weird feeling. Tired of not knowing what it was that she did to him. There was some gut *itch* there, but he couldn't figure out what it was. And that, on top of all the other things he didn't know right now, was just about enough to make him snap.

A weaker man would. But he was not a weaker man.

"I'll trust you when I absolutely have to."

"So, not at all."

"Trust is a commodity not easily imparted. If you're looking for a friend to build trust with, you shouldn't have gotten messed up in the Unsolved Crimes Investigation Unit."

"Ah, you're back to your charming self. I'll take that as my cue to go."

"Don't use all of the hot water," he called after her,

not sure why he let her get to him. She was goading him. He *knew* she was, and yet he couldn't seem to let it go.

NATALIE STOOD IN the warm pulse of the shower that was shockingly luxurious. This cabin got stranger and stranger. Parts of it were stunning in their under-stated elegance. This, what appeared to be, all glass and marble shower, the fancy pristinely white sink and floor. It was gorgeous.

But then other parts of the home were rough-hewn and distressed. She kind of liked that, actually. It was the strangest thing. It appealed to her, those dispa-rate parts.

But it hardly mattered if the decor interested her. All that really mattered was that she stop sniping at Ranger Cooper and start getting to the bottom of this mystery.

He just made it so easy to snipe.

She turned off the water and toweled herself dry. She had picked out a pair of sweatpants and a T-shirt from the closet in "her" room. It felt so completely wrong to wear someone else's clothes, somehow es-pecially since they were his sister's clothes, when all of this…hiding out was due to *her* sister. The sister Ranger Cooper didn't know might be connected to this case. She didn't think.

Maybe he'd figured it out and was pretending like he hadn't, and she was an idiot for thinking otherwise.

Or maybe the "girls" Herman said The Stallion kept didn't have anything to do with her sister.

She let out a gusty sigh. Right now she was too hungry to think about anything other than the fragrant soup that had been warming on the stove when she'd left the kitchen. It wasn't gourmet or anything, but she hadn't eaten since… She actually wasn't sure when she'd last eaten. Between the fire and the paperwork and the nervousness and fear during the drive, she probably hadn't eaten more than a few bites of food.

She hurriedly got dressed and pulled her hair back with a band she'd found in a little plastic bin under the sink. It would be a curly mess later, but she was sure this was the place where what little vanity she had left had come to die.

She had none of her normal hair products. No makeup. None of the clothes that fit her properly. While she had lost her job as a hypnotist with the Texas Rangers, thank you Ranger Jerk, it still felt like Cooper was more of a colleague than anything else. She wanted to dress professionally and be taken seriously and…

And she had to put her hair back into a crazy ponytail, and wear someone else's very nearly gaudy and way-too-tight sweats.

"Just what you should be concerned about, Natalie, how you look," she muttered to herself. She was hopeless. That was all there was to it.

She stepped out into the hall, her feet propelling her forward only because she could smell that soup in the distance.

Ranger Cooper was sitting at the table, spooning soup into his mouth as he stared moodily at a laptop screen.

He flicked a glance at her and then pointed toward the stove. "Help yourself." She gave him a little nod, and then did just that. He'd set out a bowl for her, and she ladled soup into it.

She heard a choking sound and looked back to find him nearly red and coughing.

"Are you okay?"

"Fine," he said, his voice nothing more than a scrape.

He wasn't the type of man to errantly choke on his soup. "What happened? Did you find something?" He had been staring at the laptop screen, but then there were windows in the kitchen too. "Did you see someone out a window?" She whipped her head around, looking for some clue as to what he'd choked over.

"No. No, none of that."

"Then what?"

"It was nothing," he replied, his voice returning to normal, his attention returning to his computer.

"Ranger Cooper, honestly, don't be—"

"It's the back of your...pants," he ground out.

"Well, they're not *my* pants," she muttered in return. She tried to look over her shoulder, searching for what he saw, but she didn't see anything except pink on the backs of her legs.

"It, uh, says something."

"It says what?" she demanded, flinging her arms in the air. "Do you have to be so infuriatingly vague?"

"Trust me, you don't want to know."

"Ranger Cooper, I swear to all that is—"

"It says Ride…" He cleared his throat. "Ride Me, Cowboy."

She blinked at him. "Ride…" She blinked again, a hot flush infusing her face. "I…I'm going to go change." She hurried out of the room and inspected every piece of clothing in the closet before choosing plain green sweatpants. She didn't quite love the too-tight fit, but that was far less…embarrassing than Ride Me, Cowboy being printed on any part of her clothing. Most especially her butt.

Wait. Why had Ranger Cooper been looking at her butt? He was probably just inspecting her for signs of weapons or something. There was no way that man checked out *anyone* in the course of his oh-so-important duty.

Only the desperate hunger situation coaxed her to return to the kitchen, otherwise she might have happily holed up in the strange little color burst of a room and never forced herself to have to look Ranger Cooper in the eye again.

Ride Me, Cowboy.

She shuddered, then took a deep breath before

she stepped foot into the hallway again. She was just going to have to accept that her face was probably going to be beet red for the next…eight million hours.

There are more important things to think about than a little silly embarrassment over pants that aren't even yours.

Which was a very sensible thought all in all, but it changed absolutely nothing. She was embarrassed. She was… Well, trying very, very hard not to think about riding of any kind.

She placed her palm to her burning cheek and inwardly scolded herself as she haltingly forced herself back to the kitchen.

Ranger Cooper's gaze remained steady on the laptop, but unlike the first time she'd stepped into the open front area, he was aware she was there. He didn't move, he didn't look at her, but she *knew* he was aware of her. So much different than that moment she'd caught him lost in his thoughts.

And wondered a little too hard what those thoughts might be.

"What do you know about The Stallion?" Ranger Cooper asked in that maddeningly professional tone. As if nothing had happened a short while ago, as if this was some sort of interrogation, not him protecting her. Or whatever it was he was really up to.

"I don't know what that is. A person?" Based on what Herman said, she assumed it was, but she really didn't know. It was imperative Ranger Cooper give her a hint, but she had to play that carefully. No jumping into an interrogation mode of her own.

"Yes, a person."

She finished ladling her soup and grabbed the spoon that Cooper had left out for her. She could stand here and eat it over the kitchen counter, and she'd probably be more comfortable doing that, but she didn't want to give him that kind of power over her. She wouldn't stand to eat just because she didn't want to face him.

She walked over to the table, set down her food and then slid into the seat directly across from him. His eyes remained on the laptop.

She didn't say anything because that was the technique he always used. Give her absolutely no information, even when she asked a direct question. Say only what he wanted to, and when.

So, she ate, saying nothing else, and it about killed her. She hated the silence that settled over them like an oppressive weight. She hated not peppering him with constant questions, she hated not being able to just dive in and figure out what the heck was going on.

But she didn't trust herself not to reach across the table and pummel him if he gave her another non-answer.

"Why did you question Herman?" Ranger Cooper said at last. "According to Captain Dean you always follow the rules. Never once stepped out of line. What was going on in the interrogation room that caused you to ask questions?"

Natalie didn't tense. She'd spent enough time around cops to know how to keep herself immobile and unreadable. She kept her gaze level, and when his gray-blue eyes met hers, she tried not to shudder. She tried not to feel the guilt that was washing through her. She tried to ignore all of the emotions threatening to take over, and most of all, she tried to lie.

"As a woman, I find cases about kidnappings very disconcerting." She never once looked away, because she knew that would give her away more than anything else. She stared straight into his eyes and willed him to believe her words.

"That wasn't your first kidnapping case," he said, all calm, emotionless delivery.

She swallowed before she could will away the nervous response. She had worked a kidnapping case before, but just one. It had been the abduction of a little boy in the middle of a custody battle. It had been nothing like her sister's case, and she'd known that from the beginning. "He was a small boy. I couldn't see myself as a victim."

"Herman said he keeps *girls*. Last time I checked, you were a woman."

Natalie's pulse started thundering in her wrist and in her neck, panic fluttering through her. "Obviously you've never been a young woman in a rough part of town," she returned, proud of how steady her voice sounded.

He held her gaze, but he didn't say anything. He simply looked at her as though if he looked long enough, he could unravel all her secrets.

She almost believed he could.

"What do you know about The Stallion, Ms. Torres? I won't ask again."

"Good. Because I don't know anything about him. I don't even know *what* he is. So, please, don't ask me again, because this is the truth. I have no clue." She managed to swallow down the "trust me, I wish I knew more." But only just.

"Lies could get us killed at this point. Remember that."

It struck her hard, because he was right. Some lies could get them killed in this situation, but not her lies. All she was doing was not explaining why she'd been superinterested in this case.

Her interest in the girls had nothing to do with why her house had been burned down, and had nothing to do with why she was stuck in this little place in the middle of nowhere with this Texas Ranger.

Her lie was personal, but it was…incidental almost. She didn't know anything about The Stallion or what he might be into that would make him the kind of man to kill people and burn down houses.

She reached across the table, not sure why it seemed necessary to touch him, but she thought she could get her truth across if there was some sort of connection. She touched her fingertips to the back of his hand and looked him in the eye.

"I have no intention of getting us killed. I have no intention of lying to you. All I want is to be able to go back to my life." She slid her fingers off his hand, and something shimmered to life inside of her. She didn't understand that odd feeling, and why she felt off-kilter and short of breath. Why the warmth of his hand seemed to stay in her fingertips.

So, she looked down at her soup as she said, "And if we're going to discuss honesty, why don't you tell me what you know about why we're being chased? Because I think it's a whole heck of a lot more complicated than you're letting on."

She brought a spoonful of soup to her mouth and then slid a glance at him. He had narrowed his eyes, and he was still studying her, that intensity never leaving his face.

And Natalie wondered just how long she could keep her secret…

Chapter Six

Vaughn still didn't trust Ms. Torres. There was something she was hiding, he was sure of it. Despite his absolute certainty though, he found himself inclined to believe she didn't know anything about The Stallion. She wasn't scared enough. If she knew what that man was capable of, she'd be petrified.

"There's nothing about this case that seems to directly apply to you. The Stallion is the head of an organized crime ring that deals mostly in drugs. Human and sex trafficking is also a possibility."

He noted the way she paled. It could be that fear he thought she needed, but he tended to think that the mention of trafficking didn't make people pale unless they had some sort of personal stake in the matter.

He could question her again. He could keep interrogating her until she finally gave in and told him her secret.

And he would. Yes, he would, but first he needed to finish his soup and get a few hours of sleep. That was just common sense, not caring about her feelings. He certainly didn't care about those.

"We have at least four unsolved cases we think might be connected to The Stallion and his cronies. Not to even begin to mention the current cases. Getting Herman on the leash and willing to talk was a huge breakthrough in our cases. And then you ruined my interrogation."

"You were asking the wrong questions."

"I know what the right questions are. I've been doing this for too long to ask the wrong questions. You were taking too direct an approach, and it wasn't even your job to approach anything." He gritted his teeth to stop from talking. He wasn't going to let her rile him up with her ridiculous accusations.

He finished his soup and then closed out all the files he didn't want her to have access to. He set his computer up so he'd be able to track whatever she did try to look up while he was asleep.

He didn't consider it underhanded, he considered it necessary.

"I'm going to sleep. Obviously you can make yourself comfortable, but keep all doors locked, all windows covered. You hear a noise, see anything suspicious, *anything*, you come get me immediately."

"What if someone blasts through the window and I have nothing to protect myself with?"

She made a good point, but it wasn't a particularly

comfortable one. Did he trust her enough to *arm* her while he slept? "What are your qualifications?"

Her eyebrows drew together. "My…what?"

"Do you have a permit? Training?"

"Well, no."

"Have you ever used a gun before?"

"Well…" She sighed at his raised eyebrow. "No."

Vaughn resisted rolling his eyes. Barely. "We'll see about training you, but in the meantime, don't touch a firearm. If someone comes blasting in here, they'll have you disarmed before you even figure out how to aim and pull the trigger."

She scowled, but she didn't argue. He'd count that as a win.

"If you see something suspicious, come get me. Otherwise, stay out of trouble."

Her full lips remained pressed together. The lips were distracting, but not as distracting as how…form-fitting his sister's clothes were on this woman. And thank goodness they were his *sister's* clothes and he could keep any wayward thoughts at bay with that reminder.

He turned abruptly and headed for his room. It didn't make sense to sit here sniping with her when he needed to catch a few hours' sleep. He didn't bother with a shower; he'd deal with that later. For now, he went straight to his bed and slid under the covers.

He was exhausted enough that his eyelids imme-diately closed, but he didn't drift off right away. No matter how exhausted he was, there was too much on his mind.

Unfortunately, a large portion of that was Natalie Torres. He still hadn't had a chance to dig deeper into her background beyond the file the department had kept on her while she'd been employed with them.

No criminal record. Hell, not even a speeding ticket. She'd lived at the same address for the entirety of her employment, and none of her other jobs struck him as peculiar or suspicious.

It was simply *her* that was both peculiar and suspicious. The way she'd jumped in and questioned Herman after years of following the rules. The way she'd paled when he mentioned trafficking.

The way she chewed on her bottom lip when she was thinking, leaving it wet and…

He groaned and rolled face-first into his pillow. He'd never been… He punched at the pillow, irritated with the truth. No matter how suspicious he found Ms. Torres, he was *physically* attracted to her.

Which didn't matter, of course, it was just increasingly obnoxious that the woman he didn't want to be attracted to was the one he was stuck in an isolated cabin with. For who knew how long.

But, he couldn't think like that. He had to focus on one thing at a time. If he got too worked up about what *could* happen, he'd miss something about what *was* happening, and that could get somebody killed.

He hadn't let it happen yet. He wasn't about to let

it happen now. That was how he had to think. He had to be certain that he could solve this case before any more people got hurt. But he needed to get in a couple hours' sleep so he could focus on the files and find the connection he was missing.

He needed to figure out what Ms. Torres's connection was. Because she had to have one. Maybe it wasn't with The Stallion, but she was involved with *something*. He was sure of it.

And when Vaughn Cooper was sure of something, God help the person on the other side.

NATALIE GLANCED AT the hallway Ranger Cooper had disappeared down at least twenty minutes ago. Surely he was asleep. She'd been afraid to move the entire time he'd been gone, afraid that he would somehow read her thoughts and her plan and come rushing back out and take the computer with him.

But he'd left it. Ranger Cooper wasn't a stupid man. She didn't think he'd actually have anything on that computer she could access that would give her answers, but if he had the internet, or even a basic case write-up of something, she might be able to find the information she needed to make the connection. A connection between her sister and this Stallion person.

A clue. A hint. Something, something to help her figure out how to proceed.

Natalie stood, and her heart was nearly beating out

of her chest. She had to get a handle on her nerves at being caught. What did it matter? He knew what she was doing. He *had* to know this was what she was going to do. Getting caught was the least of her worries.

Her heartbeat didn't seem to listen. It continued to beat guiltily in her chest, but she had do something. She took her bowl to the kitchen and rinsed it out. She waited after each movement to see if she could hear Ranger Cooper moving around or coming back out to the hallway. But the cabin was eerily silent.

Now her heart was overbeating for a completely different reason. The fact someone could be out there. Someone could be out there and watching her and just...

She squeezed her eyes shut and shook her head. She couldn't think like that. She could only think about survival. Thinking about who or what was after her and why...

She had to push it away, just like the knowledge her house was gone, that her sister could be dead, that her family could be in danger. She had to push it all aside and focus on what she could do.

She walked out of the kitchen and headed for the table and the open computer. She put her hand on the touchpad, and the computer sprang to life. No password to enter. No apparent security practices in place. Just an open, easily accessible computer. She glanced back down the hallway with narrowed eyes.

There was no way he would leave his computer completely unattended. Even if nothing was on here. There was something to this. Some kind of setup. Or maybe he was simply trying to prove she was underhanded.

It was insulting. He thought she was *this* dumb. For some reason that made her want to do it all the more. To do everything he thought she would do. Because it didn't seem to matter what she did, he was going to think she was hiding something. She might as well get something out of it.

It was possible her sister had been taken by The Stallion. But it was also possible her sister was taken by some other lunatic, and Natalie would never find her. But Natalie was never going to know if she didn't take this chance—regardless of what Ranger Cooper thought.

So, she pulled up the web browser and tested the availability of the internet. She cursed when she couldn't find anything. No wireless, and he didn't appear to have any kind of hot spot. So what had he been reading so intently all through lunch?

She skimmed the names of the folders on his desktop. The one on the very top was named CASE FILES.

"Oh, you really think I am just such an idiot, don't you?" she muttered, more and more insulted.

She opened the folder anyway. Maybe this was all information he didn't mind her having, but that didn't mean it wasn't worth having. It would still be more than she knew. She would take this opportunity, no matter how he used it against her in the future.

When the folder opened, there were a variety of documents inside. They didn't appear to be official police documents. They weren't reports or labeled in the way she knew cases and information at the precinct was labeled. These had to be his personal notes.

Even better.

Each file name included the words "The Stallion" plus a number code of some sort. Either his own or one outside of police work.

She began to read them in order, getting lost in the twists and turns of all the possible cases they thought The Stallion might be involved in.

It was a lot of drugs. Things she didn't know anything about. She couldn't imagine her sister had been wrapped up in drugs. Surely Natalie would've noticed that. They had been too close for Natalie to have not known or suspected that.

When Natalie got to the suspected instances of human trafficking, her blood ran cold. A lot of it was mixed up with immigration issues, but the thing that hit her hard and left her reeling was a mention of the Corlico Plant.

Her father had worked there for twenty years. He'd only stopped when Gabby had disappeared from the parking lot, waiting for him to get off his shift.

He'd never been able to go back.

And here it was, in the cases tied to The Stallion. Natalie shivered, reading quicker through the notes.

Apparently the Rangers suspected the factory of being some sort of drop-off point, or transfer station based on one raid they'd conducted, but the two women who had been freed hadn't been able to give any information that gave the Rangers further leads.

Between Herman saying he kept the girls, and this connection, Natalie was more and more convinced The Stallion was keeping Gabby. That he *had* her.

She was alive.

It was strange that the rush of tears overtook her, considering how often and how much she'd cried over Gabby. How many moments of hope she'd had that had been dashed time and time again over the course of eight years. Yet this new little tiny trickle of a lead felt like a revelation.

She'd always been certain Gabby was still alive. Her certainty had been something of a crutch, really. But there'd always been that little question in the back of her mind. What if Mom and Grandma were right? What if Gabby was dead, and Natalie had wasted her life chasing nothing?

But it wasn't nothing. This was the biggest lead she'd ever had. It wasn't proof, and maybe it was even grasping at straws, but it was something. Something had to mean everything right now. On the run, in this tiny cabin with a man she didn't understand—and was afraid she was a little too interested in understanding—she finally had a sliver of hope.

She would hold on to that for all she was worth.

She kept scanning the documents, eager to find a connection between the Corlico Plant and The Stallion.

An eerie sound pierced the air. Natalie froze. She didn't know how to describe the sound, and she had even less of a clue where it might have come from. She didn't move a muscle and strained to hear something else. Something that might identify it as harmless.

What on earth would be harmless in the middle of nowhere? Again her heart pounded so loudly she could barely hear anything, and knowing she needed to hear made it even worse. She breathed slowly and evenly, trying desperately to listen carefully. She didn't want to wake up Ranger Cooper for something stupid.

A noise in the middle of nowhere isn't stupid. It was actually probably pretty damn important. Looking a little stupid was better than being dead.

Carefully, she stood. Her legs were shaky, but she tried to walk as quietly as possible, still straining to hear something, anything, to give her a clue as to what the sound might have been.

She inched her way toward the hallway, eyes trained on the door and the windows. She didn't know whether she was expecting someone to burst through one, or one of those red dots from a laser sight to show up on her chest.

The sound didn't repeat, and she slowly moved down the hallway. Just as she reached Ranger Cooper's door, she heard it again.

It was oddly high-pitched, but not quite mechanical. Where she had originally planned to be very careful and quiet, gently waking up Ranger Cooper, the sound repeating caused Natalie to move forward clumsily and jerkily, swinging open his door with no finesse it all.

He was bolting up in the bed before the door even banged against the wall. His hand immediately closed over his weapon, which had been placed on a nightstand next to his bed.

It was the second time he'd almost pulled his weapon on her in the course of not very many hours, but she was glad he had such quick reflexes. It was oddly comforting to know he would immediately grab for his gun and try to protect them both. Considering he had never actually done anything with the gun, just placed his hand on it both times, she still felt safe in his presence.

He flung off the covers, getting out of the bed in one quick, graceful movement. He was wearing athletic shorts and a T-shirt, and perhaps a little bit later she'd have more time to appreciate just how sculpted his muscles were, but for right now she had her life to save.

"What's happening?" he asked, his hands clutching the gun at his side, looking like a man ready to fight.

"I...heard a noise," Natalie said, feeling foolish and scared and just damn lost.

He didn't balk, he didn't question her. He simply nodded.

Chapter Seven

Vaughn tried to loosen his grip on the gun. Natalie had shocked him the hell out of sleep, and the adrenaline was still pounding through him.

He glanced at Natalie's pale face. "Tell me what you heard," he ordered gruffly, shoving his feet into his boots.

"I…I don't even know. It was kind of high-pitched, but… It didn't sound like anything I'd ever heard before."

He gave a sharp nod, not bothering to pull the laces tight. "Where did it come from?" He stepped out into the hall and motioned her to follow.

"I'm not sure. It was so sudden and out of nowhere. But, it'd had to have come from closer to the front of the cabin, I think, or it would have been more muffled."

Again, he nodded. He listened for any noise aside from the sounds of their feet on the stone floor. Nothing. "I want you to stay in the hallway while I check the windows and doors." He stopped his progress and turned to face her. "You will stay right here no matter what. Understand?"

She scrunched her nose, but she didn't argue with him. She nodded, lips clamped together as though she didn't trust herself to speak.

She was smart, he'd give her that. He entered the living area, starting at the window closest to him. As stealthily as possible, he raised the curtain, surveyed what he could and then moved to the next window—each time all he saw was rocks and dusk.

He made it to the kitchen window and still nothing. They'd have to go outside. He debated making her stay inside while he searched, but it would be more dangerous to separate. Especially separating the unarmed civilian from the man trained to handle a weapon.

"I'm not seeing anything," he said gruffly, turning to find her exactly where he'd left her in the hall.

"I swear I heard something," she said, her eyes still round, her fingers clenched into fists.

"I believe you," he returned, barely paying attention as he tried to formulate a plan on how to investigate the perimeter without getting either one of them killed.

"You *do*?"

He glanced back at the note of incredulousness in her voice, focusing more on her than his plans for the first time. "Is there a reason I shouldn't?"

"No, I just…" She shook her head, looking completely baffled. "I'm...not used to people believing me. Especially *you.*"

Those last two words shouldn't have an impact on him. What did it matter if he hadn't believed her all this time? They were here, weren't they? He was keeping her safe. Yet he felt that *especially you* like a sharp pain.

But he didn't have time to dwell on that or figure it out. Quite frankly he wouldn't want to even if he did.

"We're going to have to search the perimeter together. We're going to do the same thing we did when we got here. You're going to follow me closely. Listen to whatever I say. And hopefully we'll find the source of the noise and it's nothing."

"And if it's something?"

"There are too many possibilities for us to sit here and go over all of them. You're just going to have to follow my lead, and everything will be fine."

"Is the unwavering confidence real, or do you say those sorts of things so I'll go along with whatever you say?"

Oddly, he wanted to smile. Because it was a good question—a fair one, and the dry way she delivered it. Because he appreciated her backbone. Unfortunately, now was not the time for good or fair questions. So he simply said, "Both" and then started walking toward the door.

She followed him as she had when they'd first arrived. Though her antagonism and questioning tended to grate on his nerves, he would have to give her credit for following directions when it was required.

She wanted to fight him, it was obvious, but she didn't. He admired both. Someone who didn't get a little bent out of shape about being told what to do was too much of a pushover to be of any real help. But someone who could make the choice to listen even if they didn't want to, that was a person with sense.

You're seriously having these thoughts about that woman?

He opened the door, forcing himself to focus on the task ahead and nothing else. He used the door as a shield and scanned the front yard. Since the house was nestled into one of the swells of land that wasn't rocky mountain, the land in front of the house stretched far and wide. There'd be no place to hide within shooting range, and as he scanned the land around them, he didn't see anything that might be people or the evidence of them.

The problem was going to be the back of the house. There was a small yard between the desert and the building, and walking back there would prove even trickier without having any kind of cover.

A piercing howl of a coyote echoed in the quickly cooling desert air. He always liked listening to them, but his sister had said they were as creepy as hell.

Apparently Ms. Torres agreed with his sister because her hand clamped around his arm. "That's it.

That's the sound," she said, her voice little more than a squeaky whisper.

Vaughn immediately relaxed. Dropping his gun to his side, he turned to face her. Her long and slender fingers still curled around his forearm. He glanced at her hand momentarily, not sure why such a simple touch was dancing over him like…like anticipation.

There was nothing to anticipate here. So that feeling needed to go.

"Why'd you put your gun down? What is it?" She looked at him with those wide, scared eyes, and he couldn't help but smile. She blinked, clearly confused.

"It's coyotes. We have them here, and they occasionally get close to the house and do the howling. But it's just an animal. Nothing to be afraid of."

She looked horrified, and for a second he thought he was going to have to give a lecture about how coyotes weren't dangerous and there were far bigger things to worry about, but her hand dropped and she closed her eyes. Not fear etching over her face, but a pink-tinged embarrassment.

"I feel like such an idiot. Coyotes. That's it?"

"You've never heard a coyote before?"

She heaved a sigh. "I've only ever lived in Houston and Austin. In the city. Animal noises are not my expertise. It didn't sound…howly." She shook her head, disgusted. With herself, he imagined.

"Sometimes they'll sound like a big group howl,

sometimes it's not quite so delineated, but it's definitely coyote."

"I'm so sorry," she said, all too sincerely, all too… worked up for an honest mistake. It made him itchy and uncomfortable, and irritably needing to soothe it away.

"There's nothing to be sorry about. It was an honest mistake. Unless you're apologizing for something else?"

Her mouth firmed. "No, I'm not apologizing for anything else. I… You…" Her eyebrows drew together, and those dark eyes studied him, some emotion he couldn't recognize in their depths. "But it was an animal, and nothing, and… You aren't mad that I woke you up and got you into police mode when it was nothing?"

"Of course not. You heard an unknown noise and you reacted exactly as you should have. Exactly as I *told* you to. Why on earth would I be mad?"

"I don't understand you at all, Ranger Cooper. All the things I expect you to be hard on me about, you're not, but the things I don't expect you to be hard on me about, you are."

"Then maybe you shouldn't expect either."

She laughed at that. A bright, loud laugh, and it was a shock how much the sound of someone else's laughter surprised him. When was the last time he'd heard anyone laugh? Sarcastic laughter, sure. All the time at work. But he had been so focused on getting somewhere in the cases connected to The Stallion there hadn't been any banter at work, he hadn't had any kind of social life and he hadn't relaxed at all.

It was only now, here, in the middle of the desert and mountains, with this strange woman's laughter ringing in his ears that he realized any of that. A very uncomfortable and unsettling realization prompted by a very uncomfortable and unsettling woman.

Maybe that was appropriate, all in all.

"You should call me Vaughn." He had no idea where that instruction came from. Why on earth would she call him Vaughn? He should be nothing to her but Ranger Cooper.

And yet something about that smile and laugh made him... Well, stupid apparently. "Let's head back inside."

"Your name is Vaughn?"

"No, I'm lying," he grumbled.

She laughed again as they stepped inside, and he found himself smiling. The last thing he should be feeling now was any kind of lightness, and yet that little exchange had done exactly that—lightened him. It had to be the sleep exhaustion.

"That's a very unconventional name for a very conventional man."

"How do you know I'm conventional?"

"Oh, please. You can't possibly *not* be conventional. You showed up at that fire at three thirty in the morning all neat and unwrinkled. You don't believe in hypnotism. You were nothing but…" She pulled her shoulders up to her ears and pretended to tense all over. "Like a tight ball of contained, by-the-book energy. Everything about you is conventional."

"Ms. Torres, trust me when I say that you do not know everything about me."

Her eyes met his, and he recognized that little weird energy that passed between them. He wished he didn't, but there was no denying the flirtatious undertone to all of this. He should stop it immediately.

But she held his gaze and she smiled. "Natalie. You should call me Natalie, remember?"

That uncomfortable and unwelcome attraction dug deeper into his gut. The kind of deeper that led a man to make foolish mistakes and stupid decisions. The kind he knew better than to indulge in.

But it was also the kind that tended to override that knowledge.

NATALIE'S BREATHING BECAME shallow for a whole different reason than it had the past few days. Looking at Vaughn, because he said she should call him Vaughn, and knowing they were doing a very weird, and very nearly flirting thing, yeah, it made her body respond in unwelcome ways.

She was too warm, and a little shaky. Not the kind Vaughn could see, but the kind that was internal. The kind that messed with her equilibrium.

She should really look away from that ice-blue

gaze, but she simply stared. She really should stop. Any minute now.

"You know, not believing in hypnotism isn't exactly unconventional. It's just common sense."

Well, the man sure knew how to kill a moment. She walked farther into the living room and decided to take a seat on the comfy-looking couch. Men like him never could accept there might be a softer way about getting information than torture or the like.

"What exactly do you think hypnotism is, fun? Magic?"

"That's the point. It's not magic. It's not real."

"That's because you have the wrong perception of what hypnotism is. It's not about magic. It's not about getting someone to do something against their will. It's about giving the person being hypnotized a safe place to express something that's hard for them to express. It's about finding a center, finding calm. It's not tricks. It's not getting someone to bark like a dog on stage. It's showing someone who has every reason to be afraid of talking a calmness inside themselves that can allow them to give information they, deep down, *want* to give."

She knew she was lecturing, but he was always ordering her about, so maybe turnaround was fair play. "You can't make someone do something under hypnotism that they don't want to do. The thing is, they *want* to do this. They just have a mental block. Calming their breathing and giving them that safe place gives them the tools to get over that block. It's not magic. It's not supposed to be magic. It's a tool."

He was silent for a few moments, and she thought maybe she'd surprised him with her answer. When people actually sat down to listen to how she explained hypnotism and why it worked in terms of witnesses, they tended to understand. Even if they didn't necessarily believe in it, they at least understood that no one thought this was some magical cure. *Most* people sneered at it a lot less once she explained. She had a sneaking suspicion that Vaughn was not one of those "most people."

"If they want to give us the answers, then what's the point of you? Why don't they just, you know, give us the answers?"

"Let's use Herman as an example," she replied, relaxing into the couch, crossing her arms over her chest, refusing to back down to his disdain. "He knew that he was going to die. He knew that talking to you was going to get him killed. But let's start at the beginning? How did you get Herman to come in?"

Vaughn narrowed his eyes at her and stood there for a few minutes of ticking silence. As though he wasn't quite sure that she was worthy of the information. It made her want to smack him.

"He was pulled over. Since he had warrants, he was brought in."

"And then you and Ranger Stevens decided to question him because…?"

"Because he was connected to a case that we believe has to do with The Stallion."

"So, here is this man who has a family, daughters and a sick wife. He's scared of his boss, but he also knows that his boss is doing something incredibly wrong. So his conscience is telling him to talk to the police, his common sense and survival instinct are telling him not to talk to you. When you're in that kind of moral dilemma—where you want to save yourself, but you want to save others too—it's hard to make a choice. It's especially hard to make a choice that you know will put you in even more danger than you're already in. Having something to blame your answers on is freeing. It takes the personal responsibility off you, and then you can unburden yourself the way you really want to. I would bet money that if you somehow got The Stallion into one of your interrogation rooms and I tried to hypnotize him, it wouldn't work. It only works on people who are conflicted. A part of themselves actually *does* want to talk, or they don't."

"Did it ever occur to you to tell people this before you walk into an interrogation room?"

"Did it ever occur to you to trust the order of your superior who clearly did trust me and believed that what I was doing was useful?"

"The minute I start believing someone just because he's my superior is the minute I become a subpar police officer."

"Conventional."

She thought for a second that he was going to smile. His surprisingly full, nearly carnal lips almost curved before he stopped them and pressed them into a line.

"Have you changed your mind about hypnotism?"

"No."

"Do you want me to hypnotize you?"

"No." Again that little quirk like he might smile, or even laugh.

"I bet you have some juicy secrets you're just dying to tell me."

"There will be no secret sharing, Ms. Torres."

"What else are we going to entertain ourselves with for the next few days?"

"We could discuss whatever it was that you looked up on my computer." This time he did smile, but it wasn't a particularly nice one. It was sharp edges and a little bit of smug self-satisfaction.

Ugh. Why did he still have to be hot even when he was being smugly self-satisfied?

None of that. None. Of. That. "I just checked to see if you had Wi-Fi," she returned, smiling as saccharine as she could manage.

"All the way out here you thought I might have Wi-Fi?"

"You never know."

"Why don't you be straight with me, Natalie."

"How about I start when you start." Some of that

flirtatious ease from earlier was cooling considerably degree by degree.

"I've been nothing but straight with you."

"No, you've been vague at best. Considering I'm mixed up in all of this, I really think that I deserve to know what all of this is."

"I can't put my investigation at risk," he returned, back to the implacable Texas Ranger.

"You have me in the middle of nowhere under lock and key. What risk is being posed?"

"I still don't know you. I don't know who you're connected to. I don't know what happens when you're cleared to go home. If you want to take that personally, that's your prerogative, but that's certainly not how it's meant. I don't know you, and until I do, until I know what you're after and what your connection is, there is nothing I can do to trust you. Not and do my job."

She shifted on the couch and looked away from him, because as true as it was, it was somehow still irritating. She totally understood what he was saying. It made nothing but sense, and that she was oddly hurt he couldn't trust her was ridiculous.

"I may have found a connection..." She swallowed. If she told him, he might trust her. For some strange reason, she really did want him to, but if she told him, was she putting herself at risk of never being able to touch one of these cases again? If he knew she was connected to this one little case, would he keep everything from her because her sister was involved? Or would he maybe have some compassion because he had a sister of his own?

Would it be worth suffering through having no answers to get a little bit of the possibility of a new answer? She didn't know, and she found the more she sat there and he stood there—an unmoving mountain of a man—the less she knew.

She stared into those gray-blue eyes, searching for some hint that there might be warmth or that compassion might be a word in his dictionary. There was absolutely nothing in his face to give her the inclination, and yet she so desperately wanted it to be so.

Later she would blame it on exhaustion, not just of the day, or the week, but over the past eight years. But for right now, she opened her mouth, and the truth tumbled out.

Chapter Eight

"A connection?" Everything inside Vaughn tensed as he glared at her. She might've found a connection? A connection to what? How could she have possibly found something in cases he'd pored over for years and found next to nothing except gut feelings and hunches?

"There was a case in your files…" She cleared her throat, and she most assuredly did not look at him, but she also showed no remorse for going through his files. It was hard to blame her. He would have done the same thing in her situation. That's why he'd bothered to set her up; he knew she'd do it.

What he hadn't known was that she might actually offer some information. He thought he would have to drag that out of her.

She fidgeted on the couch and chewed on her all too distracting bottom lip. He could jump all over her and demand answers, which would stop the mouth distraction, but it wouldn't be the most effective route to take.

The most effective route to take with Natalie was, unfortunately, patience. To listen to what she said, to understand it. She was a hypnotist, but her fervor over the importance of hypnotism and what it offered pointed to the fact that she was conflicted herself— a moral dilemma, just as she'd said about Herman.

So, he stood, his hands clenched into fists, his muscles held tight. And he waited.

"There was a file on human trafficking. It mentioned that there was some sort of possibility of a drop-off point being at the Corlico Plant?" She looked up at him questioningly.

He hesitated for a second, but she'd already read the file, one he'd left available to her. Might as well give her the information. "Yes, we intercepted a group of people there. Based on all the information we could collect, it wasn't the first time that the trafficking went through there. But they immediately stopped since we intercepted, and we had no one to arrest, nothing to go on. We've never been able to find anything after it."

"Three years ago, right? That's when you intercepted?"

"Yes." Three years and eight months. He didn't even have to look it up. When it came to cases he thought had to do with The Stallion, he had most of the prominent details memorized.

She took a deep breath, clasped her hands together and then straightened her shoulders. She fixed him with a certain gaze, and he knew this was going to be whatever she'd been hiding.

"Eight years ago, my sister disappeared from the Corlico Plant parking lot."

She didn't have to go further. Suddenly everything came together. Why she asked Herman about the girls, why she would ruin years' worth of work with the Rangers to ask the questions that she wanted to ask instead of letting him and Stevens handle it.

She was searching for her sister.

"Unbelievable," he muttered.

She didn't even have the decency to appear shamed. She shrugged. "Do you how many years I've been waiting to have a case that might connect to Gabby? Do you know how many hours I've spent trying to figure out what happened to her? They never found a body, in all this time. No one ever found a clue that might bring her back to us. I know she's alive. I don't care if anybody believes it or not, I *know* she is."

Her eyes had filled with tears, but they didn't spill onto her cheeks. She looked straight at him, strong and determined, and so *certain* her sister was still alive. He could say a lot of things about Natalie, but she was a strong woman. Obviously stronger than he'd even seen so far.

"Something with that factory is connected. It's too big of a coincidence. She disappeared *there*. Then Herman said he keeps the girls. The human trafficking thing stops there, and that's where she disappeared—before it stopped, I might add. It was late, and she was waiting for my father to get off from his evening shift, and maybe she saw something she wasn't supposed to see, or they saw her and thought she was part of it or…"

"Natalie, that's a lot of maybes. We have to work in fact." He tried to say it gently, but it had been a long time since he'd had to employ gentleness with someone.

"The fact is that this factory has something to do with this case. It has something to do with The Stallion. Who owns it?"

It hit him almost like a lightning bolt, painful and sharp, and he realized…

He turned to his computer and immediately pulled up the file they had on Victor Callihan. He owned the factory, and Vaughn had done extensive research into his background after the trafficking raid. He'd found nothing that might link the man to any crimes, but maybe it stood to reason to dig again, and deeper.

Callihan was a rich man. A powerful man. He'd have the means to do these things. Including keep his nose clean, even when it wasn't.

It couldn't really be that easy, could it?

Natalie was immediately behind him, looking over his shoulder at the screen. The soft swell of her breasts, accidentally he assumed, brushed his back, and he had to grit his teeth to focus on the task at hand.

"Does the name Victor Callihan mean anything to you?"

"No," she returned. "He's the owner?"

"Of the plant and the corporation that runs the plant. He's a bigwig in Austin. After the raid, we investigated him, but we didn't find anything remotely criminal. But if the plant is the common denominator, we should look into it more."

"But you don't have Wi-Fi."

"That doesn't mean I don't have wired internet." He glanced over his shoulder at her, but only came eye-level to her breasts. He quickly looked back at the computer because the last thing he was going to keep doing was noticing anything remotely sexual about her. He was too professional for that.

"First, I need to send an email to Stevens, so he can look into things from his side. He'll have access to all the Ranger files and faster internet." Vaughn tried to slide out of the chair, but again his shoulder blade kind of drifted across her breasts. Seriously. What the hell was this?

He cleared his throat and walked over to the entertainment center that held the cord he needed to hook the computer up to the internet jack. He didn't look at Natalie, and he felt like a wimpy idiot, but sometimes that was the best alternative. He certainly didn't want her to see the effect she had on him. That could lead nowhere good.

"Okay, so, what could Stevens find that might tip us off? What would we be looking for?"

"First, *you* are not looking for anything. You are an innocent bystander."

She huffed out an irritated breath. Which was better than the worried lip chewing. "I'm the one who brought this connection to your attention."

"You could have brought it to my attention a lot earlier. If you had mentioned your connection to The Stallion or this case, I—"

"I didn't know I had anything to do with The Stallion or this case. I still don't. I mean, I think it's too big of a coincidence, but that doesn't mean he has my sister. It doesn't mean..." She trailed off and looked away, and he knew that she was struggling to control her emotions.

He didn't like how easy it was to put himself in her place. Often, due to his father and sister's fame, his sister had received threatening letters or emails. Paparazzi had gotten too close, and occasionally a fan had gotten too interested. He knew what it was like to have concern for your sister's well-being.

Natalie's situation was so much worse, because for eight years now she had been in the dark. She was surviving based on faith alone. As much as Vaughn wanted to discount faith, considering you couldn't get much done with it, he couldn't ignore how admirable it was.

It was admirable that she had put herself into a position where she might find some information about her sister's case. It was admirable after all these years she believed, and she hoped. All in all, Natalie was proving to be something of an admirable woman. That was the last thing he needed right now.

"The trafficking incident was three years ago. Something could have come up in the past three years that we haven't thought to put together." She might operate on faith, but he had to operate on fact. "Knowing this little bit means that when we go back through all of that information with a fine-tooth comb. We know a little bit more about what we're looking for. And we can add the details of your sister's case with the other possible Stallion related cases. When you have a man like this, where he has his fingers in so many different things, who runs an organized crime ring, a little connection could be the connection that leads us to him."

Vaughn connected the computer to the wired internet line. She had moved away from the table, so he could sit safely at it without worrying about her body being anywhere near his.

He logged in and typed a quick email to Stevens with all the pertinent information. His instinct was to go ahead and start searching, even though Stevens would have better luck in that department. His partner would have access to all the police files at work, and faster, less frustrating internet. But when Vaughn glanced at Natalie, she was pacing the living room, wringing her hands.

He could read all sorts of emotions in her expression. It wasn't just sadness, it wasn't just fear. There was a myriad of things in there. Anger and uncertainty, hope and helplessness alike. The thing he recognized the most was that antsy kind of energy you got when you desperately wanted to fix a situation, and couldn't.

He could sit here and fool around trying to find the information he wanted, but that probably wasn't the best use of his time right now. Not if he wanted to put Natalie at ease.

Since when is putting Natalie at ease your concern?

He ignored the commentary of his brain and pushed back the chair. "I can do more searching later, but for right now we need to use what little light we have left."

She looked over at him, her eyebrows drawing together. "What do we need light for?"

"I'm going to teach you to shoot."

NATALIE BLINKED AT VAUGHN. She didn't know what to say to that. It certainly wasn't what she had expected. But she hadn't known what to expect when it came to Vaughn.

She thought he'd be angrier about her not mentioning her sister's case. She thought he'd shut her down and out while he went to work trying to find information out about this Victor Callihan. She kind of wanted him to do *that*, but Vaughn didn't do anything half-assed or foolishly, so she knew there was a rhyme or a reason to him teaching her to shoot.

She couldn't decide if she wanted to know said rhyme or reason. She wasn't sure she wanted to learn to shoot. She wasn't sure what she wanted, except an hour to have a good cry.

"We don't have too much time, so I can only show you the basics, but it wouldn't hurt for you to have an idea."

"Oh. Oh. Okay." What else was there to say?

"I'll get my extra ammunition, and then we'll go outside and get started."

"And you think we'll be safe out there?" They were inside with the windows closed, and so far he'd only let her go outside as a shadow to him. But he frowned at her, as though the question were silly.

For the first time, she wondered how old he was, considering the little lines bracketing his mouth. Actually she was starting to wonder a lot of things about him. Things that she should absolutely not wonder about the man investigating a case that might have to do with her sister. Things she definitely shouldn't be wondering about the man who was keeping her safe.

"I don't suggest things that aren't safe, Ms. Torres. Remember that."

He turned and disappeared down the hallway, presumably to get that extra ammunition he spoke of. She noticed he tended to stick with "Ms. Torres" when he was irritated with her. But when he was a little soft, or a little nice, which apparently he could be—shock of all shocks—he would call her Natalie.

She *definitely* way, way too much liked the way her first name sounded in his rough-and-tumble, no-nonsense drawl.

She really had to get herself together before she learned how to shoot a gun.

There had been a time in her life, directly after Gabby's disappearance, when she had jumped at every little thing and considered getting a gun. Even knowing her sister's disappearance was probably random, she hadn't felt safe. But in the end, the idea of carrying around a gun hadn't made her feel any safer. In fact, the idea of carrying anything that deadly when she was that jumpy only made her more nervous. So she'd never learned how to shoot and she'd never owned a gun.

But something about Vaughn was…reassuring almost. She trusted him to teach her. And teach her well. Obviously he knew what he was doing with a gun, as frequently as he reached for his.

That didn't even scare her. They were in a dangerous situation, and it had only ever felt comforting that he reached for his weapon when startled. Truth be told, nothing about Vaughn scared her. Except that nothing about him scared her. Yes, that part was a little too scary. How easily it was to trust him and listen to him and follow his orders.

She blew out a breath as he returned. He carried a box and a little black bag, and strode toward the door with his usual laser focus.

"All right. Follow me."

"Do you always express things as an order? You could ask. You could say please."

"I'm doing you a favor. I don't need to say please, and I certainly don't need to ask permission. You can follow me and learn how to shoot a gun. Or you can stay here. I really don't care which one."

She doubted that he didn't care, but she managed not to say that. Instead, she followed him outside and around the back of the house. She couldn't imagine there being much more than twenty or thirty minutes left of light, but Vaughn seemed determined to see this through.

"We're not going to worry about hitting some little target. We're just going to work with the basics of aiming and shooting."

He set the bag down and opened it, pulling out big glasses she assumed were safety related. He handed her the glasses and two little orange foam things. When she looked at them skeptically, he sighed.

"They're earplugs. You pinch the end, and you

put it in your ear. It'll keep the gun noise from bothering you."

"Right."

"Now, I'm going to explain everything before we put in the earplugs, and then I'll position you the way you need to be standing and holding the gun. Understood?"

"Aye, aye, Captain," she said sarcastically, because if she was sarcastic she wouldn't overthink the phrase "position you."

He rolled his eyes, clearly not amused by her. But that was okay, because she was amused enough for both of them.

Vaughn pulled his weapon from the holster at his hip. He began to explain the different components to her, the sights, the trigger. What kind of kick to expect and how to aim. She couldn't begin to understand all the jargon or keep up with the different things. He went too fast.

"Are you following along?"

She hated to admit it to him, and herself, but his speed wasn't the issue. Oral instruction had never been easy for her. She had to do things before she fully understood them.

"It's okay if you don't understand something. You can ask as many questions as you need to."

She hated the gentle way he said that. Hated when he was nice, because it made her feel silly or like a victim, and she didn't want to be either. She wanted to be as strong and brave as him.

"I find it easier to understand something if I'm actually in the process of doing it," she gritted, far more snappish than she needed to be.

He didn't react. He simply gestured in front of him. "All right. Stand in front of me."

She did as she was told, and stiffened perceptibly as his arms came around her sides. She had to swallow against the incomparable wave of… It wasn't just attraction, though that was the most potent thing. He was tall, a hard wall of muscle. He smelled…surprisingly good. He was warm, and she wanted to lean against him. She wanted his arms to hold her.

It's just that you're afraid and in danger. That's all. It doesn't have to mean anything.

So she would keep telling herself.

"Give me your right hand."

With another swallow, she followed his instruction. He took her hand and positioned it over the grips of the gun.

"Put your index finger here, and the rest here. Curl the thumb around." He moved her fingers exactly where he wanted them to go, and the more he did to help her put her hands in the right positions, the closer he got. The hard expanse of his chest brushed against her back.

She tried to suck in her breath and hold really still

so he wasn't actually touching her. Not because it was unpleasant, but because it was all too pleasant.

The hand not holding hers on the gun slid to her hip, and she very nearly squeaked when it fastened there. That was not…casual, a hand on her hip. Her *hip*. She could feel the sheer size of his hand, the warmth of his palm. She could feel far too much, sparkling through her.

"You want to plant your feet to maximize the steadiness of your arms. So, take a step forward with your right leg." As she did as she was told, he used the hand on her hip to position her in a slightly different way than she would have on her own.

"There," he said, his voice all too close to her ear, scratchy and, like, holy moly, sexy. Why did she have to find him sexy? Why would she think he was hot right now when he was teaching her how to use a deadly weapon?

She thought she heard him swallow, but she had to convince herself she was crazy. Someone like Vaughn would never be affected by this. He probably touched women all the time, and they didn't have any affect on him whatsoever. He probably thought of her as some kind of criminal, and that perceived swallow was all in her head.

"If you have to shoot, you want to be able to get into this position. Only in the most strident of emergencies should you do anything else."

"What's considered a strident emergency?"

"If a person is in the act of physically harming you, then you have no choice. But if there's any kind of distance between you, you want to try to get in this position. It's going to make your shots straighter and smoother. In a dangerous situation, the last thing you want to do is start shooting willy-nilly. You have to know your target, and you have to be steady."

"What if I'm shaking too hard to be steady?"

"Then you don't shoot."

"But what if someone's in danger?"

"They're going to be in more danger if you shoot when you don't have a good handle on the gun or a good stance."

"Okay. So then how do I shoot?"

He stepped closer, his body pressed to the back of hers. She knew he had to do it in order to show her how to properly shoot the gun, but that didn't mean it was easy to focus on anything but the firm warmth of a wall pressing against her. She wanted to explore it. She wanted to find out what was underneath.

Because she was ridiculous, apparently.

She took a deep breath, trying not to give away how shaky it was. But considering he was pressed against her, he had to know. He had to know that he affected her. That was so hideously embarrassing she almost couldn't concentrate.

"Now, you grip the trigger." His hand tightened on hers, guiding her index finger back to the appropriate spot.

This time when Vaughn swallowed, she had no doubt. He was affected. Granted, he was probably even more horrified by that than she was, but it was still real.

This attraction wasn't a one-sided idiotic thing. It was a two-sided idiotic thing.

"Now you're going to focus on the black spot right there on the hill. Do you see it?"

"Yes," she said, her voice giving away some of her anxiety. She hoped against all hope he thought it was anxiety over shooting a gun, not anxiety about how much her body wanted to rub against his.

"You're going to focus on the black spot. Look through the sight and clear your mind so the only thing you're thinking about is that black spot. There's nothing to be nervous about. There's nothing to be concerned about. All you're trying to do is pull the trigger while focusing on that black spot."

"Oh… Okay." Except focus sounded nearly impossible when he was all but wrapped around her. Sturdy and strong and something she absolutely had to resist.

"You can do this, Natalie," he said in her ear. "I have faith in you."

He couldn't possibly in his wildest dreams understand how much those words meant to her. How big they were even though he was someone she didn't exactly care about. Or shouldn't care about.

Still, his belief, his faith, was more than the people who were supposed to love her gave her. And she understood that. Their lack of faith and belief was mixed up in grief and a terrible tragedy. But that didn't mean she didn't miss it. She understood, but that didn't mean she stopped craving some sort of support.

So when Vaughn said it, even if he was the last person in the world she should want belief from, it mattered.

He steadied her arms, he *had faith in her*. It made her feel like she could do not just *this*, but the whole thing. That together they could find the answers that had eluded her for eight years.

"Pull," he said, and she did. Because he had faith in her. Because he had given her the tools to pull the trigger.

The gun gave a surprisingly harsh kick, but she remained steady and unshaken, even as the breath whooshed out of her.

"You hit it."

She turned to face him, still kind of in the circle of his arms, their hands still on the gun. "Why do you sound surprised? You said you had faith in me."

"Faith in you to shoot the gun, not actually hit the target."

"But you were helping me."

"I didn't pull the trigger. I wasn't looking at the sights. You aimed, you pulled, I just kept your body in position. Hitting the target was all you, Natalie."

She laughed, the surprise of it all bubbling out of

her. "You're screwing with me. Trying to build up my confidence."

"Trust me, if I helped, I'd let you know. It's not worth giving you confidence if you don't actually know what you're doing in the process."

She looked at the black spot and the little scarring inside it. She hadn't hit it exactly where she'd been aiming—right in the middle—but she had hit that black spot.

She looked back at Vaughn again, their gazes meeting. Their hands were still on the gun, and she was still pressed up against him. His hand was on her hip, his other arm curled around her other side. It was a very…intimate position—aside from the fact they were both still holding the gun—and yet she couldn't seem to make herself move.

She was pinned by that gray-blue gaze that seemed to have warmed up a little bit in the fading sunlight. Like something about the heavily setting dusk teased out the flashes of darker blue in his eyes.

His gaze dropped to her mouth, and her entire insides shivered and shimmered to life. As though that gaze meant something. As though he had the same thoughts she did—kissing thoughts. Maybe even naked thoughts.

He was so not going to kiss her, what was she even thinking? He didn't like her. He was the consummate professional. Mr. Conventional. Any thoughts about kissing were hers and hers alone, and so out of place it wasn't even funny.

"We should head back in now that it's just about dark."

"Right."

"You can…" He cleared his throat, his eyes *still* on her mouth.

That doesn't mean anything. Maybe you have something on your face. He's not wondering what your lips feel like on his, that's all you, sister.

"You can let go of the gun," he said, that note of gentleness she hated back in his voice as he carefully started to separate their bodies.

"Right." She dropped the weapon all too quickly, but Vaughn managed to catch the gun before it fell to the ground.

They were completely apart now, a few feet between them. Vaughn put the gun in his holster, not even needing to look at the gun to do so. Which, honestly, should ease her embarrassment. He was so in charge and in control and certain, why wouldn't she be attracted to that in a situation like this?

It was just…one of those things. Hero worship or something. Natural to find yourself wondering what a kiss would be like from the man who was dedicated to keeping you safe.

"We'll do more tomorrow. Of the…shooting. We'll shoot more tomorrow. Not… I mean." He cleared his throat. "We'll practice more *shooting* tomorrow."

She stared at him, something in her chest loosening. He had *stuttered*. Ranger Vaughn Cooper had just stuttered at her.

He was walking toward the house now, and she followed, but she couldn't quite stop the smile from spreading across her face.

Maybe just *maybe*, she wasn't as out of her mind as she thought.

Chapter Nine

After two days of practice, Natalie had become proficient with his Glock. She had a natural talent, and she impressed him every day.

Vaughn tried not to think too much about that. Because the more he was impressed by her, the more he felt a certain affinity toward her, and that just wouldn't do.

He'd spent half the past two days searching for information on Victor Callihan. He traded emails with Stevens about the man, but so far they were coming up empty. Clean as a whistle, an upstanding member of the community. Vaughn didn't trust it. But he couldn't deny the fact that someone else could be at the center of all this. Just because Callihan was the owner didn't mean he was the perpetrator. There were a lot of people in his corporation who could be The Stallion and thus connecting the Corlico Plant to The Stallion.

Vaughn's frustration with the case was mounting. Especially after the email from Stevens that informed him Natalie's mother's home had been burglarized while she was at work last night. Vaughn still hadn't decided whether to tell Natalie. Which was why he was currently doing as many sit-ups as he possibly could to take his mind off of the internal debate.

Natalie would be upset. She would be more scared than she already was. He wasn't sure she needed that, but he also didn't like the idea of keeping it from her. Which wasn't personal. It was his code of ethics. He didn't like keeping things from people. That was all.

Sure, that's all.

He continued to do the sit-ups, pushing harder and harder in the hopes of dulling his brain completely. He took off his shirt before switching over to push-ups.

It wasn't just trying to outexercise his thoughts. He needed to stay sharp physically as well, and the more he exerted himself, the better he slept for the short snatches he allowed himself. Which kept him better rested, all in all.

It has nothing to do with the fact that you can't seem to help fantasize about Natalie as you're drifting off.

Yeah, it had nothing to do with that.

The fact of the matter was, they couldn't stay here indefinitely. More important, he didn't *want* to stay here indefinitely. They had to get somewhere in this case so he could go back to his life, and Natalie could go back to hers—what little was left of it. But surely she wanted to rebuild. Surely she wanted to get back to normalcy. God knew he did.

He pushed up and down, and up and down, and up and down, his arms screaming, but his mind still going in circles. How did they prove there was a connection? How did they get the answers they needed? And how did he take Natalie back to Austin once their time ran out, knowing she would be in imminent danger if they didn't figure it out?

Just another case you can't solve, the obnoxious voice in his head taunted.

Did it ever occur to you that police work might not be your calling, Vaughn? I mean, really. If you need to focus your whole attention on it, and none on me, how can this be what you're good at?

He went down and stayed on the ground, more than a little irritated that Jenny's doubts were creeping into his own mind. They'd ended their marriage because he hadn't been able to give her what she wanted, but it had really ended when he hadn't wanted to fight for someone who refused to believe in his lifework. Because becoming a police officer had never been just a thing to do, or something frivolous or unimportant. It *had* been a calling. It had been something that he excelled at. Her doubts had eaten away at what little was left of the feelings between them.

"Are you asleep?"

Vaughn pushed up into a sitting position and glanced at Natalie, standing there in the opening of the hallway. She was wearing shorts today, which seemed patently unfair. Yesterday she had worn the clothes she'd been wearing the morning they left, but the day before she'd been wearing his sister's clothes again.

On the days she wore his sister's clothes, he pretty much wanted to walk around blindfolded so he didn't have to see the expanse of olive skin, or notice how the casual fabric clung to the soft curves of an all too attractive body.

Most of all, he had to work way too hard to ignore that he couldn't remember the last time he'd been so attracted to someone. And the more time they spent together, the less that was just physical.

"No. Not asleep. Just resting."

"Right. Well. I thought we could practice shooting a little bit more before you go back to sleep."

"You need to eat something. Then I thought maybe we could work on a little bit of hand-to-hand self-defense." Which was the absolute last thing he wanted to do with her—touch her. But he thought it was important. If he had to take her back to Austin without cracking this case, she needed more than a gun to protect herself. She needed every possible tool in his arsenal.

And he wanted to give it to her. He needed to make sure she was going to be safe. No matter what happened here. Even if his superiors ended up calling him back before they could figure this all out, he would consider Natalie under his protection. He wouldn't look too far into why that was. It was just his nature. He was a man of honor, and seeing things through to the end was why he was in unsolved crimes, because he didn't give up on things. He didn't walk away when things got hard.

"Hand-to-hand…self-defense?"

She sounded unsure, so as he grabbed his shirt, he tried to give her a reassuring glance, but he noticed where her eyes had drifted.

Not to his face, not to anything else in the room. She was staring at his chest, sucking her bottom lip between her teeth in a way that made him all too glad he was wearing loose-fitting sweatpants. Because no matter how hard he had to ignore that little dart of arousal that went through him, it was still *there*. Prominently.

"There are a variety ways to protect yourself," he managed to say. "I think you should know them all."

Slowly, way too slowly for his sanity and giving him way too much pleasure, her eyes drifted back up to his face. Her cheeks had tinged a little pink, and she blinked a little excessively.

She was attracted to him. Which he needed to not think about.

"So, there haven't been any breakthroughs in the case, I'm assuming?"

This was his chance to tell her about her mother's burglary. He couldn't do it. Natalie had started to relax, and she didn't seem nervous, most of the time. He didn't want to add to that. He'd tell her before they went back, but not now. Not now when she was on some kind of solid ground.

"Not so far. Callihan continues to come up clean, but we're looking more into your sister's case, and cases similar to it that are unsolved. Herman did say girls, plural."

"So, you're doing exactly what I've already been doing for the past eight years?"

He frowned at that. "You don't have the access to information that we have."

"You'd be surprised at what I found out." She laughed, but it was a kind of bitter, sad sound. And he wanted to comfort her. He could keep ignoring that want, and he would certainly keep not acting on it, but he was having a hard time denying that it existed.

"Maybe we should sit down and talk about it. You can tell me your assumptions, and I can match them with the case details."

She looked perplexed, and she stood there quietly for a few minutes while he pulled his shirt on.

"I thought you'd be angrier that I kept my connection from you."

"Just because I'm willing to help you doesn't mean I'm not angry that you kept something from me. But I also knew you were keeping something from me, so it's not as though it was some betrayal."

"Right. You don't care about me."

It was uncomfortable how badly he wanted to argue about that, but it was best if he didn't. It was best if he pretended like he didn't care about her at all. "I care about your safety."

"Because that's your job."

"Yes." Yes, that was the care. It certainly wasn't something more foolish with some woman he'd known for only a handful of days. He was too rational and practical for all that. Attraction could bloom in an instant, *care* could not.

She didn't say anything to that, but there was something in her expression that ate at him. Something about the unfairness of this whole situation... grating. It was beyond frustrating that he was now part of a case where he was not just failing, but he had to stand in front of someone who was affected by the case, and tell her, every day, that he continued to fail at solving it. That he wasn't doing his job as well as he wanted to.

"I'm not sure what I could tell you about my sister's case that you don't already know if you've seen her file."

"Why don't you tell me about *her*."

"It wasn't her fault. Believe me, I've been through every police officer who wants to say that Gabby was at fault, that she had to have done something. I have had my fill of people who want to make it into something that couldn't be helped and can't be fixed. I have no interest in doing that with you."

"Look, I can't defend every police officer that ever

existed. It's like every other profession—there are good ones, there are bitter ones. Compassionate ones, and ones who've been hardened and emptied or never had any compassion to begin with. But trust me when I say, I don't treat any case as a foregone conclusion. I don't assume things about any case. That's shoddy police work, and I don't engage in it, no matter how tempting a case might make it."

"I keep forgetting you're Mr. Conventional-by the Book," she said with the hint of a smile, but her sadness lingered at the edges.

"I have a sister of my own. She's done some really stupid things that I didn't approve of, but blame is different than being stupid."

Natalie looked away, shaking her head. "I don't want to talk about her. I don't..." She cleared her throat as though she was struggling with emotion, and he realized he was probably being an insensitive dick here, pressing her on something that hurt.

"I just miss her. It hurts to miss her, and it hurts to be the only one who believes that she *is* still out there."

"In my professional opinion, after listening to what Herman had to say, you have every reason to believe she's still alive."

"You don't think it's a long shot?"

He sighed, rubbing his hands over his face. He was walking into dangerous territory here. Comforting her when he didn't know anything concrete wasn't just wrong, but it was against his nature. But comforting her was exactly what he wanted to do. "I can't promise that anyone has your sister. I can't promise that she's alive, and I can't promise you anything to do with this case. But I think you have every reason to hope for all of those things. There's enough evidence to create the possibility."

Natalie visibly swallowed, still looking away from him. She wiped the tears from her cheeks with the backs of her hands, and it was only then that he realized she'd been crying. Again he marveled at her strength, and it took everything in him to fight the impulse to offer her physical comfort.

He got to his feet and crossed to his computer. "Let's make some notes. You and me together. We'll dissect the common denominators between your sister's case and the trafficking case."

"You know, I think I'd rather do the hand-to-hand combat thing," she said, her voice raspy.

"Yeah?"

"I've examined every detail of her case over and over and over. I can't imagine we'd find something that no one else has found. Not when Stevens knows and is looking into it too. Quite frankly, I can't stand sitting around not doing anything anymore. I'm so tired of being shut up in here. The only time I feel like I'm in any kind of control is when you're teaching me how to shoot. So show me some self-defense. Show me something that feels like I'm doing something."

As much as it surprised him to agree with her, he completely understood. There was only so much reading and trying to tie things together you could do before you started feeling useless and worthless and *actionless*.

So, he nodded at the furniture in the way. "Let's clear out the living room."

NATALIE FELT EDGY. It irritated her that part of it had to do with seeing Vaughn do push-ups without a shirt on. She had stood there watching him for way, way too long. Way longer than was even remotely appropriate. She hadn't just watched, she had ogled. But how could she not ogle him when he was *shirtless* doing push-ups in the living room? What was she supposed to do with that?

His arms had been mesmerizing. Just perfectly sculpted muscle vaguely glistening with sweat. She never would've considered a sweaty muscley guy a turn-on before, but holy cow.

Ho-ly. Cow. She felt jittery and off-kilter and kind of achy. Her one and only boyfriend had been so long ago, and she had barely thought about missing out on sex. It hadn't been a big hole in her life not to have it.

But watching Vaughn do push-ups sharply and clearly reminded her what was so great about it, and even though it was stupid, she had a feeling Vaughn would be better at it than Casey had been. Vaughn was so much bigger and stronger and gruffer and...

And then he'd started talking about cases and her sister, and on top of the achy, longing feeling, he brought up all her vulnerabilities. Talking about Gabby's case made her sad and lonely. She was a little too close to suggesting that there were a lot of ways to get rid of sad and lonely, and hand-to-hand combat wasn't one of them.

Instead, she needed to focus on feeling like… Like she had some kind of power. Like she could be strong enough to fight off any threat leveled at her. Because she knew they could only stay here for so long. If no one figured out who The Stallion was, or who'd burned down her house, she'd be in danger when they had to go back.

That scared her, but not as much as it should. She had the sneaking suspicion that even if she had to go back to Austin, Vaughn would keep her safe no matter what.

And you know that is a stupid thought.

"All right." Vaughn looked around the living room that he'd cleared. He did a quick tour of the space as if measuring it. Then he fisted his hands on his hips and looked at her.

His gaze did a cursory up-and-down as though he were measuring her up. It didn't feel sexual in the least, at least until his eyes lingered on her chest. She was wearing one of his sister's shirts, which was unerringly far too tight for her in that area. She didn't think he minded that. If he did mind, it was for a completely different reason than not liking it.

"So." He cleared his throat. "The most dangerous attacks are the ones you don't see coming. There's a certain mindfulness that you have to employ when you know you're walking into a dangerous situation. And—"

"And unfortunately my life is currently a dangerous situation 24/7?"

"Natalie." He crossed to her and rested his hands on her shoulders. "You are safe with me," he said, those gray-blue eyes nearly mesmerizing and the calm certainty in his voice even more reassuring. "Know that. My job is to protect you, and you can ask my ex-wife, I take my job far too seriously."

"You have an ex-wife?"

His gaze left hers and his hands did too. "Yes," he muttered as though he hadn't meant to share that piece of information about himself.

She hated the idea of him being married before, which was stupid, but she liked that he had given her the information against his will. That meant that maybe he had these same feelings irritating the crap out of him. All this conflicted energy. All this longing she knew she couldn't indulge in.

"Come stand in the middle of the room," he ordered.

She'd gotten to the point where she knew that when

he was ordering her around, it was because he was a little off-kilter himself.

She definitely liked that too. But she obeyed and came to stand in the center of the room.

"I'm going to come from behind. I'll wrap my arms around your upper body. And then I'll talk you through getting out of the hold."

"All right."

She stood there, bracing herself for his touch. He did just as he said he was going to do, his muscled arm coming around over her shoulders and keeping her arms almost completely immobile. Though his grip was tight, it wasn't at all harsh. It was gentle. And because she was all too antsy, and all too eager to lean into that grip, she sighed.

"You know I don't think a bad guy is going to hold me nicely."

"I'm not going to hurt you while I'm trying to demonstrate how to get out of a hold."

"How can I learn if there isn't some sort of reality to it?"

"First, you're going to learn the strategy. Then, we'll try with a little more reality to it. You need to learn some patience."

"You'll be shocked to know you're not the first person to tell me that."

He chuckled, and his mouth was so close to her ear that his breath tickled over the sides of her neck. They really needed to find out who The Stallion was, because she wasn't sure how much longer she was going to keep herself from throwing herself at Vaughn. She knew she shouldn't, hell, couldn't, and yet it was bubbling inside her like something beyond her ability to control.

"Okay, so the first step when someone has you in a hold like this is to catch them off guard. If they've left your legs mobile, then that's what you use. If you can get your elbow free, that's what you use. You're always going to want to use the sharpest part of your body and hit the most vulnerable part of theirs."

"So what you're saying is, I should kick him in the crotch?"

"Yes, actually, that is exactly what I'm saying."

It was her turn to laugh. "That's not exactly the type of thing I would expect you to suggest I do."

"When it comes to keeping yourself safe, you do whatever it takes. Keep in mind that I have a sister. I've taught her how to do this. I'm taking the same approach as when I taught her."

"You're taking the same approach with me that you took with your sister?"

It was too leading of a question, and she wished it back in her mouth the minute it had come out. But she didn't know how to sidestep the silence that surrounded them. She didn't know how to make it go away. Some silly part of her wanted to know, though. Did he think of her as a sister? As someone he would never think of sexually?

"The same approach…" He seemed to consider this carefully, and she had no business thinking that meant something. Of course it didn't mean anything. She was a lunatic reading into things. Per usual. Wasn't that her pattern?

"I guess not the same approach exactly," he said at last, some odd softness to his voice.

Her breath caught at the admission, and his arm around her loosened, just the tiniest bit. If she hadn't been looking for it, she might've missed it. But he had definitely given her more space.

"Vaughn…" What exactly was she going to say? *Look at me sexually! Please!* She was really losing it.

"If someone is holding you like this," he began, sounding uneven and uncertain. Who knew she could make Vaughn Cooper uncertain? It might be the highlight of her year.

"Let me restate the fact that a bad guy grabbing me by surprise would not be holding me like this."

"Would you like me to hold you rougher? Because I can certainly oblige." There was an edge to his voice, a warning, or maybe it was a promise. She couldn't decide.

Nor could she stop the little shiver that went through her. Because even though he probably didn't mean that sexually, it sure sounded sexual. She shouldn't poke at that. She shouldn't poke at him. But somehow her brain and her mouth couldn't get on the same page.

"I think you have to start over because I lost track of what you were talking about."

This time his grasp tightened instead of loosened, but she didn't think it was because he was trying to be a bad guy. In fact, she hoped for a completely different reason. No matter how much she shouldn't.

Chapter Ten

Vaughn was getting in over his head. He had lost track of what the hell he was doing in the first place. But he really lost track of what the hell Natalie was doing, because this was all starting to sound way more flirtatious than it should.

He tried to focus on the task at hand. With his arms around her. Why was he standing here? Because the minute he lost track of *the reason*, was the minute he started making mistakes. And he couldn't afford mistakes. No matter how good they smelled. No matter how they shivered in his arms when he said something far, far, far too suggestive.

"One of the important things to remember is that you want to stay as still as possible if someone grabs you." He forced himself to focus. To concentrate. To lecture.

She was quiet for a long humming second. "So, some strange man grabs me from behind, and I'm supposed to be calm?"

"You're supposed to try. The more you practice

this, the better off you'll be. It becomes habit. When something becomes a habit, then you can deal with things instinctually."

"So we're going to stand here with you holding me all day?"

"Well, if you'd stop talking and questioning everything I do, maybe we could get somewhere, Ms. Torres."

She chuckled at that, and he found that he wanted to laugh too. God knew why.

"You always revert to Ms. Torres when you're irritated with me."

"I'm irritated with you a lot."

"I know." But she said it cheerfully, as though it didn't bother her at all.

He sighed. Not sure why the back-and-forth banter gave him that stupidly light feeling again. The feeling he hadn't had in too many years. It revealed too much about how he'd lost himself, a fact he'd been ignoring for a while. And, more, he hated what it told him about Natalie, the effect she had on him, that it might not be some easily controllable thing.

Ha! He could control whatever he chose to. "So rule number one, what was it?"

She sighed. "Rule number one is try to stay still even though that is the opposite of any normal reaction to someone grabbing me from behind."

"Wonderful. Love the attitude," he muttered, trying to shift behind her without...rubbing. "Rule number two is, you want to analyze the situation as best as your mind allows. You want to try to figure out where the weakness is. You want to know what parts of your body have the freedom to move and inflict the most amount of damage. Obviously, if they've grabbed you from behind, you can't utilize your sight. So, unless they're armed, you want to lean back against them and try to discern the areas that are going to be vulnerable."

"So... You want me to lean back into you?"

Oh, hell. No. "Well, we don't necessarily have to practice that part."

"Shouldn't we practice the whole thing? You know the whole the more you practice, the more instinctual it becomes?"

She sounded far too pleased with herself, and he was quickly realizing how badly he'd lost control of this entire situation. It wasn't the fact that he'd initiated this stupid idea, the fact that however many minutes later he still had his arms around Natalie, it was the fact that she was goading him. She was... Hell, she was instigating.

Do not be charmed by that. Do not give into that.

But he must be going a little cabin crazy, because he wasn't sure how much longer he could listen to the sane, rational voice in his head. At some point, he was going to lose this battle. He was almost sure of it.

"Fine. Lean back into me." Yes, he was definitely losing this battle.

She did as he told her, and he tried to keep himself from softening too much into it. Because he wasn't a soft guy, and he prided himself on his ability to keep things *professional*.

So, he held himself tense and hard against the soft enticing curves of her body now leaning into him.

"How do I know if something is vulnerable?"

Her voice was a little ragged and a little whispery, and he smiled at that. Because, thank God, she wasn't messing with him without having any sort of reaction of her own.

"What's your first instinct?" he asked, his nose all too close to being buried in her thick curls.

She laughed. "I'm a woman who lives in a not totally nice area, Vaughn. Trust me, my first instinct is to go for the family jewels."

"That is the correct instinct, but you have to make sure you can get a shot. If you panic, you lose the chance of hitting a really nasty blow."

"Are you suggesting I test out a really nasty blow on you?"

"No, not at all. We can practice that move without you doing any damage."

"You trust me to practice without doing any damage? Because not so long ago you didn't trust me at all."

It was said casually, but he had the feeling there was more to it. Much like the discussion about why he was protecting her and it being only because it was his job. There was something more she was looking for, and there was something more he should not in one million years give her.

"I let you fire my gun, Natalie. I trust you."

He could feel her take a deep breath, because her back shifted against his chest. This was the danger. That they affected each other, not just physically, but in the things they talked about. In the faith and the trust that they afforded each other. This was dangerous. They were already in a dangerous situation, though, and they didn't need to add any more danger to it.

"So if someone was holding me like this, I would just reach my leg back between their legs and kick, right?"

Thank God she was focusing on the task at hand. If they could both make each other do that, maybe they'd get through this. "Yes, that's part of it. But you also want to see if you can inflict damage at the same time elsewhere. So you want to get an idea if your elbows are free. The way I've got you held right now, as long as you're not wiggling and struggling, you can get in a good elbow to the gut. If you struggle, they're going to tighten their grasp or they're going to bring their other hand around and hold your arms still, as well."

He demonstrated, which was of course also a mistake, because now both of his arms were around her, and though it was from behind, he was essentially hugging her. No matter how many times he told her what she could do to inflict damage, he was still holding her in a tight embrace.

All this *sensation* waged a war on his sanity that he hadn't faced…maybe ever. It had always been so *easy* to remain in control. Except with Natalie.

"So," he said, his voice sounding rusty and ill used in his own ears. "You want to try to lift up your leg and use your elbow at the same time. I want you to practice it, and I want you to put a little force behind it, but not too much. Especially down low."

She chuckled at that, but it was also a little bit strangled. Yes, they were both affected by this. Yes, they were both stupid. And yes, they were teetering on the edge of even larger stupidity.

Somehow, none of that knowledge made him stop.

NATALIE FIGURED SHE was shaking apart. He had to feel that, and as embarrassing as it was, she couldn't possibly stop. He was essentially holding her. This far too attractive man who seemed to have it all together when she felt as together as a lunatic.

He was *holding* her and talking to her about fighting, but the last thing she wanted to do was fight him. She wanted to turn in the circle of his arms. She wanted to press her mouth to his. The more she thought about how much she wanted that, the harder it was to ignore. The harder it was to stop herself from doing it.

But she had to. She had to stop herself. She couldn't keep doing this either, though. She had to make a choice. Either go for it, or make sure, once and for all, her mind understood that there would be no going for it. There would be no nothing. *That* was the choice she knew she had to make.

"Practice moving your elbow and your leg at the same time," Vaughn encouraged.

She laughed again, that strangled, silly-sounding laugh. How could she get her body to move the way she wanted it to when she could barely get her brain to think the way she wanted it to?

"You know, maybe we should eat something instead of all this. Or talk about—"

"Don't be a coward."

"I'm not a coward," she said through gritted teeth. "I'm trying to make a smart choice."

She felt his exhale against the back of her neck. She didn't think a shudder went through him exactly, not the way it went through her, but there was a change in the way he held himself. She couldn't tell if it was tenser or softer; she could only tell that it was different. That this was all incredibly different. She didn't know what to do about it.

"Well, I don't plan on doing this again, so you better get your practice in."

She whirled to face him, and he either let her go, or he was surprised enough by her movement that he didn't try to stop her. "This was your idea. Why won't we do it again?" Something like panic clawed through her. That he wouldn't help, that he wouldn't give her the skills he *said* he was going to give her.

She was probably never going to *be* safe, but she at least wanted some illusion of it. The belief she could shoot a gun or fight under pressure.

"You really have to ask?" he ground out. Even though she'd whirled around, they were still close. Nearly touching, really. Something glittered in his gaze, and she didn't recognize it or understand it.

"Um, yeah! Why on earth—"

Then his mouth was on hers. Just as she'd imagined far too often. All the swirling, nonsensical thoughts and feelings in her brain stopped. All the panic faded. There was nothing except his mouth on her mouth, and his hands tangled in her hair, keeping her steady under the hot assault of his mouth. All while his hard, lean body pressed against hers.

When his tongue touched her lips, she opened them for him, greedily. She threw everything she had into that kiss. Somehow she felt braver than she had learning hand-to-hand self-defense. She felt stronger than when she was shooting his gun. The kiss was better than everything that had happened to her for far too long in her life.

He was strong, and he was sure, and she wanted all of that. All of him. She wanted the way it curled inside of her, pleasure and light, breathlessness and a kind of steadiness she didn't know existed.

"I can't be doing this." But he said it against her mouth, as though he had no intention of stopping. She didn't want to have any intention of stopping. She didn't want to stop until this aching need inside her was completely and utterly obliterated.

She wrapped her arms around his neck, arching against the hard wall that was him, and somehow *she* felt powerful and in control, even as the need and desire ping-ponged through her completely and utterly *out* of control.

No matter how wrong it was, no matter how little they should do it. It was what she wanted, and didn't she deserve a little bit of what she wanted? What she wanted without worrying about if her choices were furthering her investigations into Gabby's disappearance. Her whole life had come to center around Gabby, and this had nothing to do with it except that she and Vaughn were in the same place at the same time.

Oh, and he's trying to work to help you find your sister and keep you safe.

She wasn't sure who pulled away first. She would've expected it to be Vaughn, but the insidious voice in her head that was telling her this was a betrayal of her sister and her quest to find Gabby made her pause just as much as him coming to his senses probably caused him to pause.

"I apologize. I apologize. This has gotten out of control. It is all my fault. I'm sorry. That was…"

"Really great?" she interjected, pressing her fingers to her kiss-swollen lips. Really, *really* great. Had *anyone* ever kissed her like that? With that searing intensity she didn't think... Even if that was all it ever was, she'd never forget it.

He glanced at her then, and for the first time his eyes were very, very blue. The gray had diminished, and the blue that was left was warm, and she felt like that meant something. That it *could* mean something, anyway.

"I've never..." He cleared his throat and squared his shoulders, slowly coming back to Ranger Cooper. All business, no pleasure. All by the book, conventional, Vaughn Cooper, Texas Ranger.

What a shame.

"This was a mistake. While I freely admit that I am physically attracted to you, any involvement between us could only cause problems with this case. I know how much this case means to you. It means a lot to me as well. This has gone unsolved too long, all of it, and I need to get to a point where I'm solving things. So, this can't happen again."

She chewed on her bottom lip, trying to determine how to change his mind. Except, she knew he was right. Any kind of romantic thing between them could only get in the way of this case that was so important to both of them.

She could keep flirting with him, and pushing his

buttons, and wanting more, but the bottom line was everyone involved would be hurt.

There was a selfish part of her that didn't want to care. For the first time in so long, she didn't want to *care*. It had been so long since she'd put her wants or needs ahead of someone else's, except in her want and need to find Gabby.

"Say something," Vaughn said, his voice that rough, ragged thing that shivered across every last nerve ending in her body.

Now she knew what it felt like to have that firm, unrelenting mouth on hers. Surprisingly soft, though unsurprisingly demanding. It felt like a reprieve from the harsh realities of where they were and what they had to do. The harsh reality of the possibility of this case remaining unsolved, and she could remain in danger, and her questions about Gabby could never be answered.

It was silly and awful to be concerned about a kiss. To be wrapped up in it and want more of it. Her whole focus should be Gabby until she could find her. She was closer than she'd ever been. To get distracted by Vaughn now…

"I don't know what to say," she finally managed to get out. Which was the truth. She didn't know what to say to him when so much of what she wanted was simply to forget, to lose herself in a kiss and more, and not *think* or *fear*.

At a time when they probably didn't have the luxury of forgetting much of anything. At any point someone could burst into this cabin and take out both of them. They could pretend that she was learning how to shoot a gun in self-defense all they wanted, but the bottom line was those things only worked when you had a warning, when you knew what was coming.

"You're just a little mixed up because I saved you, so to speak. It's a little case of rescue wor—"

"No," she snapped, most of the *want* cooling into irritation. No surprise he could flick it off like a switch. "I'm not stupid, and I'm not mixed up. You are the one who kissed me. I didn't initiate that. Don't insult me that way. I know my feelings, and I know why I kissed you back. It has zero to do with *rescue worship*, you arrogant jerk."

"I only meant…"

"No, I don't want to know what you meant. You kissed me. Accept that. Or should I worry that you're just mesmerized by my victimhood, and you only kissed me because you can't keep your brain intact when a victim is around?"

His mouth firmed, grim and angry. Good, because she was angry too. How dare he say that? She wasn't so stupid she thought he was hot just because he'd saved her. That wasn't what was between them at all, and she wouldn't let him get away with that kind of distorted thinking.

"I just think we don't know each other that well."

Again she scoffed. "You know, I'd love an excuse

for why this happened, for why I feel the way I do. But the bottom line is, we're attracted to each other. More, whether we want to admit it or not, we like each other. So stop making excuses. Let's deal with the reality of the situation. Isn't that what you told me? That we can't deal with what-ifs and maybes. We have to look at the facts."

"I can't tell you how little I like my own words being used against me," he returned, and though his voice had a cutting edge, there was the smallest hint of a smile on his lips.

"Especially when they're right?"

He smiled, one of those real, rare smiles that made her heart do acrobatics in her chest. He could stand to smile more. He could stand to laugh more.

You don't know him. Maybe he smiles and laughs all the time when you're not around.

But she really felt like she knew him, no matter how often she tried to talk herself out of that.

"Especially when they're right. So…"

"So, you kissed me." She squared her shoulders, determined to be an adult. Determined to take charge of her life in the few places she could. "We're attracted to each other, and as much as it pains me to say it, you're right. We don't have the time or the luxury of pursuing anything. So maybe it's best if we just pretend that it never happened."

"Right. Pretend it never happened. I can do that."

Except his gaze was on her mouth, and she didn't

think she could do that if he…looked at her with those heated blue eyes. "Maybe you can tell me all your ex-wife's complaints about you so that I know what annoyances to look for when I'm overcome by attraction."

He smiled wryly. "I think somehow you'll manage, but it's mostly your average 'you care too much about your job and not enough about our marriage.'"

"Do you agree with her assessment?" Which wasn't her business, at all, and she wanted to be appalled at herself for asking personal questions. But she wanted to know, and she'd had to gain a certain comfort in quizzing people in her pursuit of information about Gabby.

He shrugged, finally looking away from her mouth. "Sometimes. I take my job very seriously. There were times I had to miss things. There were times I was in danger and she was scared, and I get why that was hard on her."

"I feel like there's a 'but' coming."

"No but. You can't… You can't have a marriage with someone who doesn't understand your passion. I'm sure it is my failing that my passion wasn't our marriage."

"I guess that's understandable."

"I take it you've never been married."

"No, not even close. The only relationship I've really had ended because he thought I spent too much time obsessing about Gabby."

"So, great, we have more things in common. That's really what we need right now."

She had to laugh at his sarcasm. She had to laugh at the circumstances. At what the hell she thought she was doing.

But she understood what it was like to lose a relationship because you were wrapped up in something else. Something bigger than you. Something that was excessively important to you that you couldn't let go of.

"Do you regret…not changing your dedication level to police work? I mean… Would you go back and do things differently?"

"I've thought about that a lot, actually. It's been three years since she said she wanted to get divorced. The thing is, I didn't… Maybe it shows how far gone I am, but I didn't think that I was that inattentive all the time. Sometimes, certain cases got under my skin a little bit extra, but I stopped going undercover for her. I stopped… Why the hell are we talking about this?"

"I had the crazy idea that it might make me not like you."

"Did it work?" he asked.

"No, I think it might've done the opposite." She wanted to step closer again, but his demeanor kept her where she was. He had made the decision this could only be a negative distraction on a very important case. She had to respect that decision. He deserved that respect.

"I should probably get my sleep in."

She smiled ruefully. "Yeah, you wouldn't want a lack of sleep to affect your decision-making skills."

He laughed at that, a little bitterly. She almost felt bad that she'd pushed him this far. "I'm sorry," she offered to his retreating back.

He stopped and turned, eyebrows drawn together. "What are you sorry for?"

"I know you kissed me and all, but I kept pushing things, and I didn't have to. It had just…been a long time since I'd wanted something solely for myself. You know?"

He swallowed, visibly, audibly. "Yeah, I know," he said, a little too meaningfully, a little too much for her to not feel as though the stopping was the mistake, not doing it in the first place.

But he turned, in that rigid, policeman way of his, and walked down the hallway.

Chapter Eleven

Vaughn tried to sleep, he really did. He caught bits and pieces of rest, but every time he started to doze, his mind went to that kiss. The way it had rioted through him. The way his completely irrational and stupid body had taken over.

He'd had to kiss her. It had been like there was no choice. Like his life depended on having his mouth on hers. He knew that was stupid now, but in the moment it had seemed imperative.

In the moment, he hadn't been able to think of anything else except her. The easy way she kissed him back, the way everything about her seemed to fit against him in just the right way. He'd been as lost as he'd ever been in his whole entire life.

In the aftermath, he didn't know what to do about it. Apparently run away like some immature teenager was his answer. Cowardly, all in all.

But the more he talked to her, the more he wanted to kiss her again. The more he wanted to ignore everything that his training had taught him about getting mixed up with witnesses or victims or what have you. He wanted to ignore his own personal moral code and have Natalie Torres in his damn bed.

He groaned into his pillow. He felt about as frustrated as a teenager, but with the common sense of a man to make it all that much more irritating. Never in his life had he been tempted away from following his duty to the letter. Not like this. He'd always been able to be calm and rational, even when the stray thought of being the opposite had come up. He'd never gotten overly violent with a witness or perp. He'd always been calm, rational, sensible and, yes, conventional Ranger Cooper.

Why the hell was Natalie the difference maker?

After three hours of more frustrating self talk than actual sleep, Vaughn gave up. There was no use wasting time. He could be researching Callihan. He could be looking at the case. There were a wide variety of ways to employ his mind that wasn't lying there with an ill-timed erection, trying to work out why he was so affected by a woman.

A beautiful, engaging woman who made him have the most foolish thoughts. Like, maybe she…understood. The police work being a bit of an obsession thing. She had her own obsessive situation that had ended a relationship.

He got out of his bed and looked out the window. He needed to get his bearings, and maybe looking at those mountains in the distance and remembering all he'd done to get him here could help him.

God knew he needed help.

The landscape was as barren as it had been since they'd arrived. Three days now. Three days and no one had found them or come after them. As long as this kept up, Captain Dean was going to call him home sooner rather than later. And they'd found nothing. No connections, no clues, nothing to help.

He glanced at the closet where he kept the corded phone. Since there was no cell service out here, they kept a landline open in case of emergency, but neither he nor his sister cared for people being able to call them, so they didn't keep the phones hooked up.

But sometimes a phone call was necessary.

He grabbed the phone and hooked it up to the jack in the corner of the room.

The emails from Bennet were quick and usually in list form. If he actually talked to him, he might read some frustration level in his partner's tone. And, be able to ask about the time they had left without the chance of Natalie reading the answer.

Making a phone call certainly had nothing to do with having to distract himself from the gorgeous woman in the living room of his secluded cabin. Zero connection to the fact she wanted him seemingly as much as he wanted her.

With irritated jabs, he punched in the number to the office and was patched through to Stevens.

"Still nothing," Bennet greeted him, thankfully not beating around the bush.

"I figured as much," he returned on a sigh. "How much longer are they going to let me keep her out here?"

"It'll depend on the arson inspector's report. We should be getting it today. I can call down and try to speed things up."

"Yeah, I'd like to know what time frame we're working with here."

"That bad?"

Vaughn almost let it slip that it was *terrible*. But not for the reason Bennet would think. He clamped his lips together just in time to rewire his thoughts. "I don't like that we're not getting anywhere, and we might have to bring her back in the middle of it."

"Yeah, this case..." Bennet trailed off. "Without Herman, we're screwed. We've been trying to find someone he works with, someone who'll talk. Nothing."

"Nothing on those guys from the gas station?"

"They had warrants, so they're locked up, but we had nothing on him. Not who they were working for, and not what they were trying to do to you and Ms. Torres."

"I don't like this. It's too quiet, and it's too easy." Which was as true as the fact he wasn't sure how much longer sanity was going to reign in this cabin.

"I'll call Arson, see who I can light a fire under. I'll email you the full report the minute I get it."

"Yeah. Thanks."

"In the meantime, you could relax. Laugh at my hilarious jokes. Unclench."

"When have you never known me to relax?" Vaughn returned gruffly.

"That's kind of the point. There's nothing you can do. There's nothing you can change from where you are. Your only worry right now is keeping the woman safe. Which should be easy enough in the middle of nowhere. You know I'll find any more information before you do out in the desert. So, watch a movie. Make some popcorn. Have some small talk."

"I hate small talk." Especially small talk that had to do with his ex-wife, and any shared sucking at relationships.

"The point is, you can kill yourself over this case, or you can have some sense and save up all your frustrated anger into dedicated business for when it will actually be helpful to us. When you're back in Austin."

"As encouraging as ever, Bennet."

"I'm here for you, buddy."

Even though Bennet was suggesting he relax, when that was the last thing he could do, it was… Well, damn, it was nice to know someone cared enough to suggest it. But that didn't take away his ticking time bomb. "Be straight with me. How much time I got?"

Bennet sighed. "If they get something in the arson investigation, some kind of clue, you might have a few more days. But if there isn't a shred of evidence, and there never has been before, he's going to want you back right away."

Vaughn pinched the bridge of his nose, trying to ward off a headache, and swore.

"Relax. I'll do what I can to get you more time. The arson report comes up empty, I'll make sure it gets lost in red tape for a few days, best I can."

"Thanks."

"You really think The Stallion has something to do with Torres's missing sister?"

Vaughn blew out a breath. "I think it's more than possible. You?" Because he had to know it wasn't just his feelings for Natalie clouding that gut feeling.

"Yeah, man. I do. Herman talking about keeping the girls… I keep going back to that. Gotta be something there. Something that got Herman killed."

"Yeah. Well, I'll be waiting for an email."

"Later. Stay safe."

Vaughn turned to face the door of his room and then paced. He wouldn't tell Natalie anything until he had the arson report. Everything hinged on that, and he hated the idea that there would be nothing in it. Just like there was always nothing in all of these cases.

Maybe it was hopeless. Maybe they *should* head back. He'd find a way to keep an eye on her, but maybe, in the end, this had all been an overreaction. A mistake.

Then he heard the crash.

NATALIE WAS BROODING. She tried to talk herself out of the brood, but that never worked. Certainly not when there was emotional brooding, and sexually frustrated brooding, and her-life-was-a-mess-and-she-was-worried-about-sex brooding.

She should be looking at Vaughn's computer, poring over the trafficking case, finding commonalities. Anything but staring at the wall reliving that kiss over and over again. Because it *wasn't* going to happen again.

So, why not relive it if that's all you're going to get?

She pushed off the couch in a fit of annoyance. The few times her personal life interfered with her happiness, she'd been able to throw herself into the minutiae of Gabby's case. Whether it was because Vaughn was now hooked up in Gabby's case, or he was somehow that much more potent than all her other personal problems, nothing about drowning herself in her sister's case was appealing.

But what else was there to do in this godforsaken landscape? She was stuck in this cabin while Vaughn soundly slept in his room. Jerk.

She glared down the hallway as if she glared hard enough, he might feel her ire. Not that it would matter. He wasn't going to do anything about it, was he?

And neither was she, because the sleeping jerk was right. So torturing herself over it was downright—

She heard the distant sound of…something, so incongruous to the quiet she'd been living in for the past days. Though the sound immediately stopped, Natalie knew she'd heard something, and it wasn't coyotes this time. Whatever the sound had been, it was distinctly mechanical. Like a car.

Before she had a chance to even think about what to do, she was already moving toward the hallway, moving toward Vaughn. But a sudden crash caused her to jerk in surprise so violently that she stumbled. She fell to her hands and knees and looked back at the front of the house where the crash had come from.

The sound repeated, and she saw the door shake just as Vaughn entered the hallway.

"Stand up and get behind me. Now."

She scrambled to her feet and did as he ordered, the grim set to his mouth and the icy cold in his gaze crystalizing the fact this wasn't a *mistake* or a random animal this time. Fear jittered through her, much like it had in the gas station when she'd been at the mercy of those strange men, and all she could do was shake and listen to Vaughn.

He had his weapon drawn, and the minute she was close enough, he jerked her behind him.

"No matter what happens, you stay behind me. Got it?"

"But—" She could think of a hundred scenarios

where she would have to not stand behind him, but before she could voice any of them, another crash shook the door. She had a feeling that it would only take one more harsh blow for it to open.

"What are these morons doing?" he muttered. He held his gun at shoulder level, but his other arm was extended behind him, keeping her in the box of his arm and the wall.

With absolutely no warning, he spun and shot his weapon, right over her shoulder. A thud sounded, and then a wounded grunt, and when Natalie caught up enough with the whirlwind of action and looked behind them, she saw a large man's body slumped on the floor.

"Diversion," he muttered, grabbing her arm and pulling her toward the man's body.

Vaughn kept her behind him as he approached the man who was gurgling and thrashing and reaching for a gun he'd apparently dropped. Vaughn kicked it out of his reach easily.

"Pick it up, Natalie. Train it at the front door. Anyone walks in, you shoot."

Natalie tried to agree, to nod, but she stood there shell-shocked and shaking, and—

"Natalie." This time Vaughn spared her a glance. "You can do it. You have to do it. All right?"

It steadied her. Not that she stopped shaking or stopped being afraid, but it gave her something to

hold on to, something to focus on, and she managed
to grab the man's gun with shaking fingers.

"Put your back to mine."

"I don't—"

"Turn around, look at the door and lean your back
against mine. From here on out, you don't move unless I do. We're always touching, unless I say otherwise." He said the command low, and the man flailing
about on the floor probably could have heard it, but
he seemed pretty preoccupied with the bullet wound
in his shoulder.

Natalie blew out a breath and did as Vaughn instructed. She pressed her back to his, absorbing the
warmth and the strength, and focused on the door in
the front of her. The crashing seemed to have stopped,
but she held the gun up, hoping she'd be able to shoot
an unfamiliar weapon. Hoping harder she wouldn't
have to shoot anyone.

"Who the hell are you?" Vaughn growled.

Since Natalie was watching the door, she couldn't
see what the man did in response. But it sounded like
the man merely spat in response.

"You'll regret that one later."

Natalie couldn't suppress a shiver at the cold note
of fury in Vaughn's voice.

Another crash sounded, and the front door shook
again, but Vaughn seemed less than worried about
it. She, on the other hand, was *more* than worried
about it.

"What are you after?"

The man only groaned, still not saying anything.

"This is your last chance to talk. You don't talk when I ask, I don't ask. And you don't want to find out what happens then."

The man only cursed, and Vaughn remained a still, calm, rock-hard presence behind her. His warmth and his strength soothed a small portion of her concern over her too fast and hard breathing.

"Natalie, link arms with me." He held his arm back, and she did as he ordered. Then he was maneuvering her, always keeping her protected from the man on the floor.

He led her by her linked arm into his room, keeping his gun trained at the wounded man. He'd stopped writhing and was looking increasingly pale, though he kept his hand on the wound on his shoulder.

Natalie looked away.

"I need you to grab the backpack out of my closet. It's black, and it should be very heavy."

Natalie swallowed, and she didn't trust her voice. But she did what he asked. Vaughn's closet was freakishly neat and tidy, so it was easy to find the backpack.

"Is there anything you absolutely without a shadow of a doubt need from your room?"

She had so few belongings left, tears stung her eyes thinking of leaving any of it. But she also didn't want to, oh, die, so she supposed she could do without. "My ID, maybe? Unless you don't think we have—

His mouth firmed. "I don't want to leave behind anything that might give them more information on you. We're going to link arms again. We're going to get your ID. Do not look at the man on the floor. Keep looking straight ahead until we're inside, and then grab your stuff immediately. Then we'll go out the window. Or at least try."

"And if we can't?" There could be fifty men surrounding the cabin as they spoke. There could be—

"One thing at a time." He maneuvered her across the hall, his grip firm enough to help her push away the thousands of terrible outcomes.

"Go," Vaughn said gently, unlocking their arms. Because she couldn't have come up with a thought on her own to save her life, she went straight for her purse.

It was strange how unmoored and that much shakier she felt without Vaughn's arm connected to hers, but she pressed on. She grabbed her purse, and Vaughn, keeping his gun trained on the door, rummaged around in the closet and pulled out a backpack. It was pink and sparkly and utterly ridiculous.

He gave it a disgusted grunt but held it out to her. "It'll be easier to get through the mountains with your hands free instead of worrying about a purse. Shove it in there and then strap it on your back."

Again, Natalie couldn't trust her voice to actually

come out of her throat, so she simply did as she was told. She shoved her purse into the outrageous backpack and then strapped it to her back. Meanwhile, Vaughn pulled on his backpack.

She looked down at her hands, the gun she held, the power she had. This was her protection. This would give her a chance. She hoped.

"You hold on to that. No matter what. If it comes down to it, you'll use it."

"What are they after?" she asked, her voice a shaky, squeak of a thing that would've embarrassed her if she'd had time for it.

He didn't bother to answer. She understood that he didn't have time to stand there and explain things to her. But she couldn't help the fact that she didn't understand anything about this. Not a thing.

"Keep your eye on the door. Keep your gun ready."

It took every ounce of focus and control to do as he said and not watch what he did. She heard the rustle of curtains, and possibly the squeak of the window. Meanwhile, all she could do was watch the door to this room, and fervently pray that no one tried to walk through it.

A shot rang out, and Natalie jerked violently. Through some lucky twist of fate, she didn't pull her own trigger.

"Follow me. Now." Vaughn's voice was terse and urgent as ever, and her feet responded to the order even if her mind whirled.

Though a million questions went through her head, she followed Vaughn out the window. It was only then that she realized there was a sound louder than the harsh flow of her breathing.

Once she was outside, she noticed there was another man slumped on the ground. But he was screaming and grabbing his leg. Vaughn paid him no attention. He was too busy scanning the surroundings.

"Stay at my back."

She was glad he kept saying it, because in her shell-shocked state she would've forgotten. She would've stood there still and silent and barely functioning. This might be the only situation in her entire life where she was *ecstatic* for someone to keep reminding her what she was supposed to do.

She stayed at Vaughn's back, mirroring his movements as he walked toward the screaming man. Vaughn spared him the most disgusted of glances, and then grabbed the large, intimidating looking gun that had fallen out of the man's reach.

"How many more of you are there?"

"Screw off."

Vaughn's mouth was a harsh, grim line. "So none. Perfect. Now, when you crawl your way back to your boss, tell him the next time someone comes after me, it better be the man himself. Because his lackeys are damn bad at this." Vaughn gave the man a swift kick in the chest so the man fell backward, screaming all over again.

Then Vaughn started walking, and Natalie had to remind herself to follow him. It wasn't hard. Not when he exuded calm and confidence and *safety*.

He went to the front of the cabin and there was nothing that she could see, but Vaughn jerked his chin at a vehicle in the distance. "That's where they parked their car. We'll go in the opposite direction in case there are more shooters coming."

Natalie looked in the opposite direction. "But it's just…mountains."

"I hope you're ready to camp, Nat. Because God knows how long we're going to be out there."

Chapter Twelve

The sun was beginning to set, and Vaughn knew he needed to find a place to camp. But the adrenaline still pumped through him, and the last thing he wanted to do was stop.

He looked back at Natalie, who was...struggling. Struggling to keep up with his pace, and he thought maybe struggling to keep her composure after such a whirlwind of events. He was being an ass for not caring more about what she felt, about the toll this was taking on her.

"It's just a little bit farther. There is a series of caves up here. They'll make good shelter for the night."

"Caves?" she asked, trepidation edging her voice.

"It's perfectly safe if you know what to look for."

"What do you mean, 'if you know what to look for'?"

"Just... Trust me."

"I don't think I have a choice," she said, sounding

exhausted and like she was in a little bit of shock. He couldn't blame her.

Maybe if he distracted her she might make it the last little distance they needed to travel. "You didn't happen to recognize any of those men, did you?" Because interrogating her would be distracting. He made such *excellent* comforting choices.

"No, did you?"

"No. And with no cell service, I can't call in a description to Stevens." He glanced up at the quickly fading light. It was a stunner of a sunset, pinks and oranges, a riot of colors. But how could he care about beauty when he was worried about Natalie?

Which was a problem he didn't have time to consider.

He found the entrance to a cave that looked suitable. Luckily, he'd been exploring the area around the cabin since he was a teenager. He'd been dedicated to making it a safe space for his sister, and he'd spent a considerable amount of time figuring out what that would take. Which meant he had spent some time camping in these very caves, hiking all these mountains.

Unfortunately, he didn't have the equipment he usually had, but he was a Texas Ranger. He knew how to make do.

"So you think more people are after us?"

"Two teams of two so far. I imagine if that piece of trash takes my message back to his boss, we'll see an escalation."

"Do you think he will? Do you think The Stallion would really come after us himself?"

"I don't know, but I'm tired of dealing with his lackeys." Which was an understatement. These weak attacks were practically an insult.

Though the diversion of the man trying to break in the front while another snuck in the back had almost worked. Way too close for comfort.

Natalie inhaled and exhaled, loudly. Fear and exhaustion evident in every breath she took at this point.

"Let me double-check this cave. As long as I don't see evidence of…" Noticing the wariness on her face, he didn't finish his sentence. She didn't need to know what creatures might lurk in the caves. It was best she knew as little as possible.

"Stay put for a few minutes. Keep your eyes on the horizon."

She nodded, and as he ducked into the cave, he couldn't fight the wave of admiration he felt toward her. She didn't argue with him, she didn't get too scared to move. She did what he asked, and he was able to relax enough to trust her to handle some of it.

Not everyone could do that. Hell, there were some kids who couldn't hack it in the police academy with as much poise as Natalie had showed. Even scared as she was.

He did a quick survey of the cave. They wouldn't go very far in. Just enough to have shelter from the elements. There were no signs of predatory wildlife at this particular point, and he'd have to hope that held out for the night.

He returned to Natalie at the opening of the cave, noticing the way she looked around the mountains. Wide-eyed. Awed. Afraid. He wished there was something he could do to keep her mind off of all that was going on around them.

You know what you could do.

He ruthlessly shoved that troublesome voice out of his head and focused on the task at hand.

"I don't have the gear I normally have to camp, but I have this emergency pack, and it'll get us through."

"What if someone finds us?" she asked, those wide brown eyes settling on him. He had to push away the stab of guilt, the harsh desire to comfort her at any cost, with any words, with any touch.

But it wouldn't serve either of them to lie to her. "We have three guns and a tactical advantage, and we'll be watching for them."

She nodded at that and stepped inside the cave with him. He took off his backpack and nodded at her to do the same. He started to rummage for something he could put down so she could try to rest, or maybe some food, but he noted that she was shaking.

He didn't know if it had just started or if she'd been doing it the whole time, but he found a sweat-shirt from his pack and handed it to her.

She shook her head. "Unfortunately it's not cold,"

she said with a self-deprecating laugh. "I just…can't seem to stop."

He swallowed, because his first instinct was to pull her into a hug. Quite honestly, even if he wasn't attracted to her, that would be his instinct. As a police officer, he knew how powerful it could be to simply offer someone a shoulder or a brief, simple embrace. It could give them the courage to make it through a really tragic situation.

Which meant he had to swallow that attraction, and act as though she were anyone else. Anyone else he would offer this to. So he stood and thrust his gun to his hip holster, where it would remain in easy reach. He took the gun she'd been carrying all this time from her shaking fingers and set it behind them. If they showed up, the shooters from the cabin would be unable to sneak around them, and the weapon would be within easy reach.

He steeled himself for what he knew would be a shock of arousal and need, and drew her into the circle of his arms.

She shook there, and he thought she might have cried. Just a little bit of a sob. Against his shoulder. It was strange to feel capable in that moment. To feel like the Ranger he'd been trained to be.

But for the first time in a long time, with Natalie in his arms, he felt in control of the situation. Because he would do anything in his power to protect her.

And that was going to be everything.

NATALIE DIDN'T LOVE that she was crying, but it couldn't be helped. It wasn't like she was going to get any privacy to do it any time soon.

Might as well get it out now while there weren't people directly after them. Just indirectly, at some point, in the future. Probably. Did they have another few days? Or were they going have to camp in the mountains for weeks?

She couldn't bring herself to ask Vaughn any of those questions because he always answered them either far too truthfully, or not at all. So she focused on evening her breathing and getting rid of the tears, and finding that inner strength that had gotten her this far.

As she slowly calmed herself, she realized that Vaughn was rubbing his hand up and down her back. It reminded her of the night of the fire, the way he'd put that competent, strong hand on her back and it had been an odd comfort. But it hadn't been personal.

This felt *personal*. Intimate.

She wasn't crying anymore. No, she was absorbing. The strength and warmth of Vaughn, his arms around her, and the gentle, soothing motion of his hand up and down her spine.

It didn't make camping in a cave any more appealing, but it made it a little less daunting. Vaughn would keep her safe. That she knew.

She sighed, and relaxed. Into him, into the embrace. He didn't stiffen against it. Instead, he softened. Vaughn Cooper softening against her. She smiled and burrowed in deeper. Holding him closer.

"I'm going to get you out of this in one piece," he said, his voice a fierce whisper. "One way or another."

"Are you supposed to make impossible promises like that?" she asked, listening to the steady, reassuring beat of his heart.

"I shouldn't," he said, sounding a little disgusted with himself. "But you should know that I'm going to do whatever it takes. I know I can't tell you not to worry, but I can try to give you some comfort."

She looked up at him, still in the warm embrace of his arms. She smiled, and it was odd that she *could* do that in this situation, but something about his fervent need to make her feel safe, made her feel just that. Maybe safe was an exaggeration, but she felt like there was a chance they'd survive this. A good one. Because she trusted Vaughn to do exactly as he said.

"How much distraction would it be if you kissed me?"

Some of that softness left him, a tension creeping into the set of his body. "Natalie…"

She wouldn't be so easily deterred. "I'm just saying that if you want me to feel safe, that would probably do it."

He exhaled something like a laugh.

Then he did the strangest, most unexpected thing. He actually kissed her. Lowering his mouth to hers, something gentle and sweet. The antithesis of the hot and wild thing that had passed between them earlier.

This was a comfort, and that made her heart shudder with things she had no business feeling. And yet, she didn't want to stop feeling them.

She wrapped her arms around his neck, deepening the kiss, pressing herself more firmly against him.

His arm pulled her tighter to him, and one hand came up to cup her neck. The warmth of his hand there, the pressure of it, the heat of his mouth and the way his tongue traced her lips and then entered. It was soft and comforting, but it was also more. It was hot and searing. It was a revelation, because she'd never had anything like this. It was fire and sweetness, it was passion and comfort. It was everything she wanted, and all she'd had to do was ask.

She stroked her fingers over his short hair and then down his neck. She wanted to somehow know him. The shape of him. The feel of him. She wanted to understand the texture of his hair, the path of his skin. She wanted more.

That hit her. She wanted more. She wanted it all. She didn't care that they were in a *cave* somewhere. She didn't care that horrible people were after her. Because everything had been going wrong for so long that she just wanted more of this thing that didn't feel wrong.

She wanted good. She wanted Vaughn.

She trailed her hands down his chest. The soft cotton of the T-shirt he wore did nothing to hide what compact, lean muscle he was. Everything about him was hard. Strong. But she thought maybe, just maybe, there was some softness under there. In the way he wanted to protect her, in the way his mouth explored hers.

Even if there was no gentleness in him, he used his strength as a kind of softness. He was a protector, and that was his gentleness. She admired that. Deeply.

"Natalie…"

He didn't have to speak further, she could feel him pulling back, if not physically, mentally.

She clutched him tighter, not willing to let this go. She'd sacrifice her pride for this. "No, don't."

"For every minute we spend doing this, we are putting ourselves in danger. Every minute one of us isn't watching the cave entrance and paying attention to our surroundings, we are increasing the danger that we are in. Exponentially."

"I don't *care*." She knew that was stupid, but she couldn't bring herself to care. Her care was worn out and afraid and *tired*. "We're already in danger, what's a little more?"

She trailed her hand farther down his chest, across the clear indentation of his abs, doing something far bolder and more brazen than she'd ever done. Something she almost couldn't believe she was doing herself.

She placed her palm over the hard length of his erection.

He groaned, sounding tortured and desperate. She

smiled, not minding making him tortured or desperate in the least.

"My job is to keep you safe. I can't… Do that…"

"Right now I want your job to be to make me forget. I want to forget I'm scared. I want to forget my life was burned to the ground. I want to forget that I'm on the run and in danger. I want to forget that my sister's missing and there has been nothing I could do about it for years upon years. Vaughn, I want to forget. Let me forget."

She traced the hard length of him, and his grip on her tightened.

"It would be a dereliction of my duty…"

"Derelict with me. Please." She stepped back from the tight embrace of his arms, and he let her. Probably thinking that that was going to be it. That she had come to her senses. But that was the absolute last thing she had come to. She pulled the T-shirt over her head and tossed it toward the backpacks on the ground.

"Natalie." His voice was all gravel, but his eyes were hot and on her.

"I want you, Vaughn. I don't care where we are, what it takes. I want this, and it's been so long since I've had anything I wanted."

She could tell he was fighting a war with his conscience, so she did her best to win it for her side. She shimmied out of the shorts she'd been wearing. Because the ground was rocky, she left her shoes on. It was probably a ridiculous sight, her in her underwear and tennis shoes. Based on Vaughn's tense reaction, she thought she was getting her point across, though.

He took a step toward her, and because she couldn't quite read his expression, whether he was going to insist she put her clothes back on or possibly do it for her, whether he was going to give in to touch her, she held out a hand to stop him.

"No, no, no. Lose your shirt and pants first."

He stood there, a solid wall of granite. The fact he was even standing there, even debating, was a triumph. It was a win.

He clenched his fingers into fists and then relaxed them, and they went to the hem of his shirt. She exhaled the breath she'd been holding. She was fairly sure that as he lifted his shirt over his head, she whimpered.

He was… Perfection. He had abs and muscles and was just this powerfully broad man whose impressive upper body narrowed to mouthwatering lean hips. She wanted to trace each cut and dip. Possibly with her tongue.

"Pants too," she said, though it was really more of a squeak than her voice.

Again there was a moment of pause. As though he couldn't believe he was doing this. But that didn't stop him. Thank goodness, it didn't stop him. He undid the button of his jeans and then the zipper and pushed them down. Underneath he wore a loose pair of black boxer shorts, but as loose as they were, she could still see the evidence of his arousal. She could see everything. And he was gorgeous and perfect and she wanted nothing more than to be underneath him. Or on top of him. Or both, alternating.

"Am I allowed to approach now?" he asked, the gravel still in his voice, but a hint of humor underneath.

She opened her mouth to say yes. In her mind she said the word regally and coolly. As though she were in control of the situation, as though she were in control of the rioting sparks inside her. In reality, nothing came out of her too-tight throat, and she just had to nod.

When Vaughn grinned at her—at *her*—nothing else mattered. Not the danger they were in, not what might happen afterward. All that mattered was him and now.

He took a step toward her, but his hands didn't reach out to touch. He stood so they were still a couple inches from being toe to toe. He looked at her, right in the eye. It felt more intimate than standing there in her underwear. The fact that he was looking at her, seemed to look *into* her. That was… Somehow huge and emotional.

"We're going to move a little deeper into the cave. That'll be a safer option. We'll have more of a warning if something happens."

"Remember when I said you were so very conventional?"

"I'm a *man*, Natalie. But I am a man determined to keep you safe, no matter what."

"Are you at least also a man determined to make love to me, not just take off his clothes?"

For the first time since this whole thing had gone wildly out of control, he didn't hesitate. "Yes. More than determined."

It was her turn to grin, and she helped him gather all of their stuff, and even though they were each holding weapons and had backpacks strapped to their bare backs, bundles of clothes in their arms, he held her hand.

He led her farther into the cave, having already pulled the flashlight out of his pack. She tried not to think too deeply about him searching every nook and cranny, and what might be hiding in any of those little places. But he found a little…corner almost, that gave them something like a wall between them and the opening of the cave.

"It'll keep us out of sight, but you're going to have to be quiet."

She giggled at that. How had they gone from running from men with guns to…quietly having sex in a cave?

"What a shame."

"The only shame is that I can't see you."

Those words clutched around her heart and her lungs. She could scarcely suck in the breath to tell him that… She didn't know what she wanted to tell him. She didn't recognize this overfull feeling in her chest. Excitement and lust or something more? She wasn't sure she wanted to delve too far into that possibility.

So she simply held her arms open for him, and he stepped inside. His mouth took hers, his body took hers, and she gave. Everything she had. In a way she never would've imagined. But knowing she had so little, and there was so much against her, it made her open up in a way she's always been scared to.

Because for the first time in her life, she really had nothing to lose. Okay, maybe her life, but she wasn't so sure she was in control of that.

This, she was in control of. Or at least partially in control of.

Vaughn's hands touched her gently and reverently, as though he was trying to find just where she like to be touched. Just where to stroke to make her forget where the hell they were.

In a cave. On the run. Giving themselves to each other. She couldn't think of anyone she'd rather give herself to, and she had the sneaking suspicion that had very little to do with the danger they were in.

Chapter Thirteen

There was the smallest voice in the back of Vaughn's head telling him to stop this madness. But Natalie was nearly naked, all smooth skin and tantalizing curves in the not-at-all-sufficient flashlight beam. Everything about her was like a soft place to land, and the last thing he should be doing right now was landing. He should be leading and fighting and protecting.

But the driving need of his body had taken over. He wanted Natalie as his. No matter how he tried to tell himself that it was wrong, or the wrong time, or some other combination of those things, it got lost somewhere. Usually about the time he had to actually consider taking his mouth from hers, or his hands from her body. He couldn't stand the thought.

Especially when her mouth was so sweet under his, and her hands were so determined to explore him. She seemed to touch every piece of him. A finger traced the scar on his shoulder from a stab wound he'd gotten undercover. She poked her finger into the dip of his hip. But the most brain melting was the fact that she kept arching against him, a slow, sensuous rhythm that made him completely crazy. Incapable of thinking of anything else but being inside her.

He had no business thinking that or wanting that or most especially doing that. At this point, he didn't know how he'd ever stop.

He undid the snap of her bra and slowly drew the fabric down her shoulders and arms. He exhaled, surprised to find it shaky. Surprised to find how much she affected him.

"Are you cold?" he murmured as she shivered now that she was bare from the waist up.

"No," she returned.

"Are you scared?" he asked, rubbing his hands up her arms, trying to infuse some calm, some surety.

"No." This time she said it on a laugh. "It feels good. All of it." Those dark, meaningful eyes peered into his. Her smile was like the gift of sunshine after weeks of darkness. Perhaps months or years, because he had been unwittingly, unknowingly in a period of darkness. Something about Natalie lightened him, even in the middle of all this mess.

"So, I don't know how much you're going to want to hear this, but I happened to see a packet of condoms in your sister's backpack when you handed it to me. So… You know."

He squeezed his eyes shut. "Can you rephrase that in a way that I don't have to think about the fact my sister has condoms in her backpack?"

"Why? Do you think she's too young to use them?"

"No, regardless of whether she should or not, the last thing I want to consider right now is my sister having sex. Period. With anyone. Especially in the cabin that we share."

"Okay. New story—I just love carrying condoms around in my purse."

He laughed, and shook his head. "I just haven't…"

She raised her eyebrows, and he realized this was a conversation he did *not* want to get into right now. Right here. It was too close to a truth he was still trying to bottle up. The fact he hadn't slept with anyone since his ex-wife.

The fact he hadn't wanted to, that he'd thrown his life into police work just like Jenny had always accused him of.

That wanting this, Natalie, here, now, it all *meant* something.

But there was too much at stake for that meaning to be dissected in the here and now. "We'll have plenty of time to converse after. Let's not waste our present."

"Take off your underwear, and I might be inclined to agree with you." She grinned, all jokes and fun in the midst of this awful situation for her.

"Grab a condom from *your* purse. I'll lay out some blankets."

She gave a little nod and bent over the pink sparkly backpack. Vaughn focused on the tempting curve of her backside over *where* she was obtaining the condoms from. When she turned back to him, she cocked her head.

"Where are the blankets?"

"Sorry, I was distracted."

She smirked and rolled her eyes. "Then I guess turnabout is fair play. Please bend over and retrieve the blankets," she said with a regal lift of her hand.

He chuckled, but he did exactly as she asked. She made a considering sound, and he didn't waste any time retrieving the blankets. Both pieces of fabric were lightweight backpacking blankets that wouldn't do much to protect Natalie from the harsh, hard ground, but it would keep them from rolling around in rocks and dirt.

Rolling around in rocks and dirt. While armed and dangerous criminals were probably after them. "Are you sure—"

"I simply won't take no for an answer, Vaughn," she said primly. "Don't make me say it again."

He promised himself he wouldn't. He would make sure they both enjoyed this. That they would get everything they needed out of it, and when they had to face whatever they had to face tomorrow morning, they would do it together. Both having had this moment. This coming together.

He crossed to her and took her mouth. No preamble, losing some of the gentleness that had held him back earlier. He wanted. She wanted. It was time to take—and give.

She moaned against him, arching in the way that drove him crazy. He slid his fingers into her underwear, finding the soft, wet heat of her. Stroking and exploring until she wasn't just shaking in his arms, but shuddering. Panting. Desperate.

And he was desperate too.

"The ground is rough. So I'm going to lay on my back, and you're going to get on top."

"You just lay out orders everywhere you go, don't you?"

But she didn't protest when he lay down and pushed his boxers off his legs. Not a complaint, just a steady gaze at the hardest part of him illuminated only by the flashlight he'd rested on the ground. "I believe that means it's your turn to take off your underwear."

She grinned at him and shimmied out of her underwear. She knelt next to him and handed him the condom. He opened the packet and rolled it on himself, watching her as she watched him. She licked her lips and he groaned aloud.

"How on earth are we going to do this?" she asked, and though it seemed like she *attempted* to make eye contact, her gaze never made it very far.

"Just figure out however you feel comfortable."

She straddled him, that intimate place of hers not making contact with his body. She trailed her fingers down his chest and his abdomen. He could only barely make out the tight points of her dark nipples, only barely make out the seductive shape of her body.

But she was here, straddling him, those smooth legs brushing up against his sides, her scent, her warmth permeating the very air.

"Are you sure you're comfortable?" she asked before chewing on her bottom lip in that sexy and distracting way she did whenever she was worried.

"Baby, all I feel is you." Which was true. When it was all said and done, he might notice the way the rocks dug into him, but for right now, all he could see, feel, think, want was her.

She leaned over him, her breasts brushing his chest, her lips brushing his mouth. "Then take me," she murmured.

It was his turn to take the order, and he did, sliding home on a moan, moving deep and steady, paying attention to the way her breath caught and exhaled. The pleasure and excitement coiled so deep and so hard, he wasn't sure he'd ever survive.

His hands dug into the softness of her hips, but he let her set the pace. Slow and tentative at first, and then she moved faster, everything about her softness, her breathy moans, *her* driving him closer and closer to that reckless edge.

She was beautiful, moving against him, sighing, gasping as she chased that rhythm that would lead to her release. It bloomed in him, big and hard, something more than where their bodies met.

She said his name, pulsed around him. He thought he could make out the way the flush in her cheeks had spread across her chest as she sighed out her release.

But it wasn't enough. He pushed himself into a sitting position, pulling her legs around him. Her gaze met his, glazed with pleasure.

"Again," he ordered.

And when she opened her mouth to protest, he covered it with his own.

AGAIN. THE HARSH, demanding way Vaughn had said those words echoed in her head. Again? She'd just lost herself over some edge she'd never known, how could she possibly do it again?

But he was kissing her, using that harsh, steady, hot grip on her hips to pull her forward. She arched against it, against him. She loved the way her breasts scraped across his chest. She loved the way his hands were commanding and sure. She loved this. Being with him. Being filled by him. Being driven to some sort of climax that was bigger than she'd ever known.

She was starting to think it might be a dream.

But Vaughn kept moving, urging her to take more of him, and then less, over and over again in a steady, unrelenting rhythm. The blooming edge of pleasure began to build again. The heat that should've been unbearable, but she couldn't stand to lose. A fire in her veins that she didn't want to be cooled.

He broke the kiss and his mouth streaked everywhere. Her cheeks, her neck, her chest. He was everywhere, driving her into a faster and faster pace. She could feel his desperation grow, the closeness of his own release, just thinking about that, of being with him, finding that pleasure together, it pushed her over that last humbling, bright edge.

Vaughn held her there, deep and strong, his harsh groan echoing in the expanse of the cave.

She wasn't sure how long they sat there wrapped up in each other, holding on for dear life. She wasn't even sure how long the orgasm pulsed through her. She didn't care. In this dark cave with Vaughn, it didn't matter what time it was. All that mattered was that he was holding her, that he was a part of her.

"You're shaking again, and I think it's cold this time," he murmured into her ear, so gentle and sweet.

It was hard to think she could be cold, but as he grabbed a sweatshirt and pulled it over her head, she realized he was right. She was shivering with cold, *among* other things.

The sweatshirt he put on her was his, oversized and warm, and it smelled like him. Clean and soap and Vaughn. She wanted to snuggle into that smell and him forever.

"We should get dressed."

If he hadn't kissed her forehead and her cheek and then her neck before moving, she might have been fooled by that tense note in his voice. But he was so gentle, and affectionate, and she realized that his tenseness wasn't about what had passed between them, it was just that he was coming back to the job he had before him.

He was dedicated to her safety. He was dedicated to her. She couldn't help but be warmed by that.

She rolled off him and tried not to watch with too much interest as he got rid of the condom. He handed her a pair of pants that would be too big, but they would keep her warm. The cave was much cooler than the outside air.

"You can change back into your clothes tomorrow when we set out. The sweats will be too big to move in, but the shorts and shirt won't be enough to keep you warm tonight."

"Have you always been such a good caretaker?"

"I guess it depends on who you ask."

"I'm asking you."

Those inscrutable gray-blue eyes met hers in the eerie glow of the flashlight beam. Something in his gaze shuttered, and she realized this was quite the sore spot for him. "You've done nothing but take care of me so far," she said firmly, wishing she could erase those doubts in his eyes.

"That's my job."

"It's more than that."

"Do you want to rest, or do you want to try to eat something first? All I have are some granola bars and some jerky."

"Vaughn, I want to talk."

"We can talk about whatever you want, except about my caregiving tendencies."

She frowned at him as he got dressed. He seemed to have an endless supply of things in that black backpack of his. She sat on the blankets that he'd stretched out, dressed in his clothes, watching something like irritation make his shoulders hunch.

"So, is this the part where you're just certain that I'm going to look at you like your ex-wife looked at you?" she asked, perhaps too bluntly, but if she was going to have ill-advised sex with the man, she was going to ask him too-blunt questions.

If her life was in danger, she was going to push where she normally wouldn't. She was going to demand what it would never occur to her to demand in her real, unassuming, obsessed-with-Gabby life.

He faced her, and in the light everything about him seemed hard and unreachable. Granite she'd never be able to push through. Except she had. She *had*.

"We had sex once, Natalie. I like you, I do. But you're nothing like a wife."

It was a nasty thing to say, and it hurt even though she knew it shouldn't. She wasn't his wife, she wasn't even close to his wife. She'd be lucky if there was anything they could salvage after this whole ordeal.

But just because words were designed to hurt, no matter the truths or lack of truth behind them, didn't mean that she could let it go.

"I'm not trying to be an ass," he said on a sigh,

rubbing his jaw. "But don't make me into something I'm not."

"I'm not making you into anything. I'm reflecting on what I've seen from you, and if you can't accept that part of yourself, that's fine. Don't take it out on me."

"I'm not big on sorry." He said it with such a grave finality she opened her mouth to tell him he was a jerk, but he kept going.

"But I'm sorry. Because I was feeling guilty for letting my personal feelings interfere with this case, and I took it out on you, and that's less than fair."

Her heart ached for him then, because she knew that she'd initiated this. She'd pushed for it. Not that Vaughn hadn't wanted it or hadn't enjoyed it, but it had come at a cost to him. It required him to bend that ironclad moral code he lived by, and that meant something, not easily distilled no matter how great the orgasm might have been.

It was crazy to think she might love him. She barely knew him. And yet everything in her heart said that love was what this feeling was. Love, or the seeds of it. There was so much possibility, and yet so much against them.

"Apology accepted," she said, hoping her voice sounded light rather than as ragged and rocked as she felt.

"Just like that?"

"This wasn't a mistake, but I understand why it

might be hard for you to accept. But I'll never regret it. No matter what happens."

"You say that now…"

"And I'll say it always. No matter what." She stood, because she needed to somehow prove to him that she was strong. That she meant it. "That was what I needed, at that exact time I needed it. And you gave it to me. Nothing you could do could take that away. Nothing that happens changes what you gave me."

He stared at her, and she thought she saw some pain there, and she assumed it probably had to do with his marriage that had dissolved. No matter how much or how little he'd given, that relationship had clearly left scars. She wished she could sew them together, kiss them, make everything okay.

But she couldn't. And not just because they had dangerous men after them.

"Let's eat something, and then one of us can try to sleep."

He kept staring at her for a few humming seconds of silence. Then slowly, oh so painfully slowly, he crossed to her. He touched her face, his blunt fingertips tracing the lines of her cheekbones and then her jaw, then her neck. His eyes bore into hers, and her heart hammered against her chest.

She wanted to say silly things like I love you, and she knew she couldn't. She absolutely couldn't.

"For the record, I'll never regret it, either."

When he kissed her, it was gentle, and it was sweet. And Vaughn Cooper gave her something that no one else had for a very long time.

Hope.

Chapter Fourteen

Vaughn managed a few hours of sleep, after he watched Natalie sleep for far too long. It had been tempting to lie next to her, to wake her with a kiss. So, he'd done neither. He'd stood guard the entire time she'd slept, and then he'd woken her by nudging her with his foot.

Because he was a bit of a coward, all in all.

Though his brain and body were nothing but a swirling mass of confusion he didn't have time for, exhaustion won out and he slept quick and hard.

Natalie woke him at the first sign of dawn, just as he'd instructed, and then he began to pack everything.

"Are we going back to the cabin?" she asked him, trepidation coloring her every movement.

"No. We're hiking farther."

"Until what?"

"I know the area well enough to lead us toward civilization. Somewhere our phones work and we can call for help. It's too dangerous to go back to the cabin."

"But what about your truck?"

"They slashed the tires," he returned. He hadn't wanted to tell her all the things he'd noticed as they'd escaped from the cabin. That they took care to not shoot anyone, that they'd snuck their way into a position to *take* not murder.

He supposed murder would be scarier, but the idea of Natalie being held by those men… He wasn't going to let that happen.

"When did you notice that?" she asked incredulously.

"When I kicked Worthless Number Two over, I saw the tires were flat." And that the man had been carrying handcuffs and rope. Duct tape. Vaughn swallowed at the uncomfortable ball of rage and fear in his gut.

Natalie blew out a breath. "How long will it take to get us back to civilization?"

Vaughn pulled out the map of the Guadalupe Mountains that he kept in his emergency pack. He'd studied it last night while Natalie was sleeping, but he was worried and thorough enough to look at it again.

He inclined the map so she could see too. "This is the path we're going to follow." He showed her with his finger the mountains they would have to cross to get inside the national park and finally find service or a ranger station to assist them. "I don't know exactly where we'll get cell service, so we just have to keep going until we get it. Or find someone who can help us. My hope is that they don't expect us to keep moving forward this way, and it'll give us enough of a head start that by the time they realize it, we'll be close enough to call for help."

Natalie chewed her bottom lip and studied the map. "Do you have enough supplies to get us through all of this?"

"It'll be tight and we'll be hungry, but we'll survive."

"You don't know the meaning of sugarcoating, do you?"

"Do you want me to sugarcoat it?" Because he would, if that's what she wanted. He wasn't sure who else he'd afford that to.

She sighed again, pulling her hair back in a ponytail. It stretched the tight T-shirt across her breasts, and he had to stop himself from wondering how much he'd be able to see if they indulged in each other right now. In the pearly light of dawn easing its way into the cave. Her skin would glow, she would—

They didn't have time for that, and even if he'd lost his mind once, he couldn't do it again. At least not if it meant wasting daylight. Maybe tonight...

He shook his head and told himself to focus. "First things first, we're going to start moving toward higher ground. Hopefully that gives us a tactical advantage, and we can see if anyone's following us before they catch up."

"What do we do if they are?"

"Well, that depends on how close they are. We'll either book it, or we'll pick them off. But that's a lot of what-if, Natalie."

"You shot those other men. Do you think…" She swallowed, and he didn't know if it was her conscience or something else bothering her, but either way that was something that she was going to have to work out on her own.

Every officer who vowed to protect the innocent and took up a weapon had to come to terms with what that meant and the power it offered. They had to come to grips with what they were willing to do. He couldn't convince her of his morality or his lack of guilt, and, in the next few days should she have to use her weapon, only she could deal with the aftermath of that. He couldn't do it for her, no matter how much he'd like to.

Because if he had the choice, he would save her from every hard decision. Which was another thing in a long line of things he didn't have the time or energy to think about right now.

"It was my intention to give them non-life-threatening wounds, but without medical attention, it's hard to know if they survived, and quite frankly I can't concern myself with it. The only thing I can concern myself with right now is keeping you and me safe."

She didn't say anything for a long while, and he let her be quiet as they walked out of the cave. They would need to make it to another shelter by nightfall, and though he could read the map and do some general calculations, he couldn't be sure where they'd end up when the sun set.

So, they needed to head out and get as far as they could. He didn't think they could make it to cell service today, but if they got good enough mileage behind them, they could hopefully get there tomorrow.

They hiked in silence for most of the morning, and though Vaughn was sorry that she was obviously brooding about a difficult situation, he couldn't feel bad that there wasn't any conversation to distract him from his task at hand.

Occasionally they stopped and ate a snack and drank some water. Vaughn would consult the map, but mostly they walked. He knew she was exhausted, and probably on her last legs, but he also knew that she was strong and resilient, and that he could push her and she would survive. That was one of the things he most admired about her.

"You're holding up remarkably well, you know," he said as they sat on rocks and Natalie devoured a granola bar.

She glanced at him, the granola bar halfway to her mouth. Her gaze didn't bother to hide her surprise. "I haven't really had a choice, have I?"

"We always have a choice. One of the choices is to lie down and die, to give up. One of the choices is to think that you can't, and so then it's a self-fulfilling prophecy. You could be so busy complaining about the lot you've been given that we never got anywhere. But you've chosen to move forward. To keep fighting. Not everyone could have done that, not everyone has that kind of wherewithal. I'm not sure anyone should *have* to have that kind of wherewithal, but it's special. And you deserve to know that."

She smiled a little and looked down at her granola bar for a second before leaning over and giving him a long, gentle kiss. Her arm wound around his neck, and it took all the willpower he had not to lean into that, not to pull her into his lap. He couldn't let her distract him, but…

She pulled away, that sweet smile playing on her lips. "You know Vaughn, I like you a lot. That's not something I would have said about five days ago."

He chuckled a little at that. "Well, that's very mutual."

It was her turn to laugh, but she sobered quickly. "When we get back…" she began, emphasizing the *when* meaningfully. But her seriousness morphed into a grin. "You're going to have to let me hypnotize you."

He narrowed his eyes at her, but he couldn't help from smiling in return. "Like hell, Natalie."

"Why not? Are you afraid?"

"No. You told me that the person has to be willing. I'm never going to be willingly *relaxed*. Unless it's by things other than hypnotism."

She snorted at his joke. "Do you have secrets to hide that you're not willing to share, Ranger Cooper?"

"I don't have any secrets." Which had become true the minute they'd discussed his marriage. There was nothing about himself kept under wraps, because there wasn't much there. Work.

She might not know he was related to a few celebrities, but that wasn't *his* secret in the least.

Natalie looked down at the last bite of granola bar, something in her gaze going serious. "I guess I don't really have any more secrets from you, either." Her eyebrows had drawn together, and she didn't look at him. "Everything in my life has been Gabby for so long…"

She swallowed, and Vaughn could tell she was dealing with some big emotion, so instead of pressing or changing the subject, he gave her time to work through it.

"I want her back so much, and I just *have* to believe she's alive… But…" She shoved the granola wrapper into her backpack forcefully, irritated. "I feel terrible saying this, it feels like a betrayal, but when we make it out of here, I want a life that isn't solely focused on her." Her brown gaze met his, and he had a bad feeling he knew where this was going.

And where it couldn't *possibly* go. Because his feelings for Natalie ran very deep, but he'd been here before—loving someone and knowing that her views on the world would never allow them to make something permanent, to make something real.

"One step at a time. Remember?"

She frowned at him as though she could read his thoughts, as though she could read everything. He didn't like that sensation at all. But in the end, he didn't have to bother figuring it out because a shot rang out in the quiet, sunny afternoon.

Immediately Vaughn had Natalie under him, protecting her body with his, scanning the horizon for where the shot might have come from.

"Wh-where?" Natalie asked in a shaky voice.

"I don't know." Based on the sound, he didn't think it had come from behind them. It seemed more likely it came from higher ground. From someone who'd presumably assumed his plan all too easily. He swore viciously and tried to reach for his pack without leaving Natalie vulnerable.

Another shot sounded, a loud crack against the quiet desert, this one getting closer. It had to be coming from the other side of the mountain they were climbing. They couldn't stay put, they were too vulnerable, too exposed. And he had no idea where to shoot toward.

"We're going to have to run from it," he said flatly, his eyes never stopping their survey of their surroundings.

"Run for it? Run where?"

He pointed to a craggy outcropping a little ways

behind them. "You run there. No matter what happens to me, you run there and get behind those rocks."

She tried to twist under him, but he wouldn't let her. "What do you mean no matter what happens? You can't honestly expect me to—"

"The most important thing is that you stay safe. Out of the way of a bullet. If I—"

"What about you? What about your safety?" she demanded, a slight note of hysteria in her voice.

"Natalie, listen to me," he said, his voice calm, his demeanor sure. Because not only was it his *job* to take a bullet for her if the circumstances necessitated that, but he wanted to. He'd never be able to live with himself if she ended up hurt because of an error in his judgement.

"My job is to keep you safe."

"Well, Vaughn, I want *you* to be safe too, regardless of what your job is."

He'd analyze the way those words sliced a little later. "I'll be safe. If you listen to me, we'll both be safe. We're going to make a run for it. You first. I'll follow."

"I don't like this."

"Unfortunately, Nat, it doesn't matter what you like, this is what we have to do."

She exhaled shakily, and it wasn't until she spoke that he realized it was anger not fear. "If you get shot," she said, her voice trembling with rage, "I will finish off the job myself. Do you understand me? You will not get hurt saving me."

Everything inside him vibrated with a kind of gratitude and hurt and all number of things he couldn't work out at the moment. He kissed her temple, which was the only place on her head he could reach.

"You just listen to me, and everything will be fine. I've gotten you this far, haven't I?"

"Yes, and I know you'll get me the rest of the way. We'll get each other the rest of the way."

He hated that she was worried about his safety. Her safety was of the most importance, not his. He was a man who could be replaced easily enough, but there was no one like Natalie.

But if she cared about him, and her safety depended on his, then he would keep himself safe. He would keep them both safe.

"On the count of three, we run. That's our destination. If I happen to get hit, you keep going. You can't save me if you're dead."

"And you can't save me if *you're* dead," she argued.

Another shot rang out, and Vaughn knew that one was way too close for comfort. The next one would hit, and if they weren't trying to kill them, all the more danger.

"One, two, three, go." He launched to his feet, pulling her with him, and then they ran.

NATALIE RAN, JUST as Vaughn instructed. There was a certain hysteria bubbling through her, but with a specific destination—behind that rock—she managed to focus enough to get her feet to move, as fast as they possibly could.

Another shot rang out, and Natalie jerked in fear and surprise and almost tripped at the sound, but Vaughn's steady grip on her arm propelled her forward. She tumbled behind the rock, and Vaughn was right behind her, covering her with his body again.

As glad as she was to have someone protecting her, someone like Vaughn, so sure, so capable, worried about her safety, she had fallen in love with the man, and she hated the thought that he was ready to give his life for hers.

She knew this was his job, but that didn't make it easier. Certainly not easier to know he was risking his neck for her. She didn't feel worthy of it. She didn't feel worthy of any of this.

Why were these men after *her*? All she'd done was pathetically fail at trying to find her sister for *eight* years. Failure after failure. Why on earth did they think her worthy of this kind of manhunt?

Now was not the time to worry about those questions, about her failures, but every insecurity, every pain, every hurt seemed to center inside her along with this bone-deep panic.

Vaughn made an odd grunting sound as he rolled off her. She glanced over at him, and he was trying to pull off his jacket. She didn't quite know why he was bothering with that when—

"I'm going to need your help," he said, his voice strangely strained.

"What's wrong?" she asked, despite the way her throat tightened. Something was off, something—

Then she saw it, the angry streak of red in the middle of a rip on the T-shirt fabric across his shoulder. She felt like *she'd* been shot, seeing that horrible gash and the way the blood trickled down his beautiful, strong arm. For her.

He spared her a glance. "Not going to pass out, are you?"

"No," she said firmly, though she did feel a little woozy and light-headed at the sight of him bleeding so profusely, but she wasn't going to be so weak she couldn't help him. She would find a way to push through her physical reaction and give him everything he needed.

"Tell me what you need me to do."

"Grab something out of the backpack that you can wrap tight around the wound." He had his gun pulled and was holding it with his good arm. Ready to take a shot. Ready to protect her in the middle of this barren mountainous desert. "I can do it myself if you want me to—"

"I can do it." Natalie would do whatever he asked, whatever he needed. Over and over again.

He kept his gaze trained on the area around the

rock that protected them. Natalie did her best to hurry to find something she could wrap his arm with. She hoped this was at least a little bit like in the movies, because then she would at least know a little bit of what to do.

There was a T-shirt at the very bottom of his pack, and she pulled it out. Without thinking too much about it, she pulled and pulled until she ripped a good strip. She repeated the process over and over until she had several strips. While Vaughn remained the lookout, she folded the strips over the worst part of the wound and then tied the longest one around his upper arm as tight as she could manage.

He hissed out a breath, but that was the only outward sign that he hurt.

"That should hold for little bit," she said, scared and worried that she'd screwed it all up. But what could she do? All she could really do was everything he asked, hoping for the best. She had no other options here, so there wasn't even a point in worrying about what else there was. Like Vaughn kept saying, there was only now. No time to worry about later.

"On the slim chance that we have a signal, check your phone and mine."

Natalie scrambled for both, powering them on and checking their screens. But there was no service. She wanted to cry, but she blinked back the tears. Tears would get them nowhere.

A shot hadn't rung out in a while, and the longer

the silence lasted, the more both their nerves seemed to stretch thin and taut.

"Pull up the texting on both phones. I want you to put in a message to this number, and hopefully if we try to send it now, it'll send the first second we have service without us having to keep checking."

Natalie furiously typed the information Vaughn gave her. She kept glancing at the T-shirt bandage, and because it was a white T-shirt, she could see the blood already seeping through. She tried not to panic at that.

"Get out the map." Though he still sounded like cool and collected Vaughn, that strain never left his voice.

He'd been shot. *Shot.* It took everything she had to pull out the map and spread it out for him. Her hands shook, but he still handed her the gun she'd dropped while trying to bandage him up, trusting her. Believing in her. She held on to that fiercely.

"Shoot at anything that moves."

She swallowed and nodded, watching the harsh surroundings and fervently hoping nothing moved.

"We don't want to retrace our steps," he muttered. "We need to keep moving forward. We've got to keep searching for cell service. We don't get out of this without help."

She wanted to make another joke about him not sugarcoating anything, but her voice didn't work anymore. Whether it was panic or fear or some combination of all of the emotions rioting through her, she couldn't push out joking words. Only desperate ones.

"Are they going to come after us?"

"They might. I didn't get a glimpse of where they were coming from. I still have no idea what the hell they're trying to prove. If they want us dead, they could have had us dead on the road before the gas station. I don't get this at all, unless they want us. Alive. Or..."

He didn't have to finish that sentence, and she knew, sugarcoating or no, he wouldn't. Because he meant *or they want you.* She could tell that bothered him more than anything. That he didn't know what they were trying to do, that she might be the target.

Natalie didn't really care what they were trying to do. As long as they were shooting at them, she wasn't a fan.

"To keep cover we're going to have to backtrack a little bit, but then we'll circle around, really try to get higher ground on the off chance there's a tower around here somewhere. If you hear the message sent notification from either phone, tell me. Otherwise we need to stay completely silent, just in case. They don't want us dead. Or at least they don't want you dead, and that's pretty damn frightening."

"But..."

For the first time his glare turned to her, rather than their surroundings or the map. "What the hell do you mean, but..."

"If they have Gabby..." She swallowed at the lump in her throat. Maybe they wanted her too. If they did...

"No. No way in hell. You're not sacrificing yourself for her right now. First of all, not on my watch. Second of all, because you just told me you want a life beyond all that."

"I didn't know how close I was."

"I'm sorry. I know she's your sister, and I know you'd do anything to find her, but it's been eight years. If she survived that, a few more days won't hurt her. You don't know what they're trying to do to you, so we're not taking that chance. Not even for your sister, Nat."

"You'd do it for your sister," she returned, quiet and sure. He'd sacrifice himself for less, she was certain.

"It would depend on the situation, and not in this one. If they had my sister, I'd do exactly what I'm doing now. Which is trying to get them. Because if we don't have them, everyone under their control is in danger."

She saw a point to that, but the idea that if they took her she might be reunited with Gabby. If they took her... Vaughn might be safe.

"Natalie, you have to trust me on this. I need you to promise me."

Natalie swallowed. She hated lying to him, but she also knew they wouldn't get anywhere if she didn't make that promise. She forced herself to look him in the eye—those gorgeous blue eyes she thought she'd never be able to read—and now she knew she'd never not be able to see what was in those depths.

He was strong and he was brave, and he knew that he could get them out of here. But he was also afraid, because whether he was going to admit it, whether he would admit it, he cared about her too. He wouldn't have slept with her in the middle of all this if care wasn't part of that. That she knew.

"All right. I promise," she said, holding on to the thought of care, of love.

Vaughn swore harshly. "Don't lie to me." He grabbed her arm and winced a little, since he'd used his bad arm. But he didn't back down. "I don't have time to argue with you on this, but if you put yourself in danger you will answer to me. Now, let's go."

He didn't give her a chance to argue; he pushed and pulled her in the direction he wanted to go. And Natalie let him lead, let him order her around.

But she had no doubt if the situation presented itself, she'd sacrifice herself for both the people she loved.

Chapter Fifteen

Vaughn didn't know what to do with the searing rage inside him. She was lying. How dare she lie about something so important? How could she be willing to sacrifice herself with so many unknowns and so much at stake? She didn't even know for sure if her sister was alive or with The Stallion. All they had were hunches and possibilities, and Vaughn was beyond livid that she would take such a chance with her life.

It didn't matter that he would do everything in his power to make that impossible for her, because it wasn't about him. It wasn't about what he could do. It wasn't about how well he could keep her safe. It was about the fact that she was *willing*. It was about the fact that…

She should've cared more about herself. She should've cared more about her future.

Which does not include you, so maybe calm down.

Frustrated with himself, more than frustrated with the situation, he pushed them forward at a punishing pace, doing his best to keep them behind things that would keep them out of sight and safe from bullets.

But even as they hurried and zigzagged and did their best to stay low, Vaughn could hear the sound of an engine getting closer and closer. He swore, because no matter how good he was, no matter how strong he was, no matter how smart he was, he could not outrun a vehicle. He couldn't outrun whatever was coming after them.

They'd made it around one of the craggy desert mountains, and whatever was coming for them would have to come around one of the sides. Vaughn kept his weapon drawn and his eyes alert. "We're going to find somewhere to hide you."

"But—"

"No but. You will listen to me. You will follow my directions. If I tell you to hide, you will damn well hide." He didn't have time to see how she was taking that harsh order. He didn't have time to look at her and make sure she was okay. He was a little afraid if he did take that time, he'd fall apart.

He'd been in some dangerous, uncomfortable, scary situations, and he'd never been scared that he might fall apart. It poked and ate at him. Hell, it just about killed him that she'd become that important. Which meant the only choice was to keep going.

He found a very small opening, more crevice than cave, in the base of the mountain. With less finesse than he might have had otherwise, he gave her a little push into the crevice. She fit, though barely. But it would keep her out of sight.

He looked around to make sure he couldn't see a car anywhere. He could hear that engine, so they were close, but not close enough to see him just yet.

"Stay here. No matter what. You do not come out of here until I come to get you. Someone tries to get you out, you shoot him wherever will do the most damage." He didn't even have time to ask if she understood. He gave her one meaningful look and tried not to let those big, soulful brown eyes undo him.

He didn't have time for that, or to ascertain whether she would listen to his order. He could only keep moving. Because if he stayed there and the vehicle came around one of those bends, they would know exactly where to find Natalie.

Vaughn took off running as fast as he could, ignoring the screaming pain in his shoulder. His heart was pounding and his breath was scorching his lungs, and he had the sinking suspicion it had more to do with the fact that he'd left Natalie alone than with the fact that he was running.

He slowed his pace, took a quick look at his surroundings. He could still see the crevice where he'd pushed Natalie, but he couldn't see her. He was far enough away that it would take a lot of searching for anyone to find her.

Now he had to figure out which direction he wanted to go to, and—

The sound of a gunshot made Vaughn skid to a halt. He glanced around, trying to ascertain where the sound had come from. There were little craggy outcrops all over the desert. There were cacti and other plants that a stealthy person might be able to hide behind. Vaughn searched and searched, but he didn't see anyone, or anything.

The sound of the engine had stopped, and he did his best to keep his gaze everywhere rather than always on where Natalie was. He didn't want to give it away, because who knew what these men had. They could be watching him with binoculars, they could have an army of cars. They could have anything, and he didn't know.

He couldn't think about the what-if. He had to think about the right now.

"Ranger Cooper."

Vaughn whirled to see a man walk out from behind the opposite curve of the little mountain. He appeared to be alone, but Vaughn wasn't stupid enough to think that was true. Any number of people could come pouring from the other side of the mountain. There could be an *army* of men behind the curve, and that was daunting, but it couldn't stop what Vaughn had to do.

"Mr. Callihan, I assume?"

The man laughed and spread his hands wide, though Vaughn noticed that the gun he carried was pointed directly at Vaughn's chest regardless of the gesture.

"It took you only how many years to figure that out?"

"A lot fewer years than it will take me to kill you."

The man kept walking closer and closer, and Vaughn's hands tensed on his gun. He could shoot the man and be done with it, and there was a very large part of him that wanted to. But he resisted, because his mission wasn't to kill every bad guy who roamed the earth; it was to bring them to justice.

He believed in justice, and while he believed in using his weapon with deadly force if necessary, as long as this man wasn't actively trying to kill him, or take or harm Natalie, Vaughn was having a hard time rationalizing shooting first.

Maybe some of it had to do with the fact this could potentially be the only man on earth who knew where Natalie's sister was. If Vaughn killed him without trying to retrieve more information, what might Natalie think of him? What might she lose?

It was the absolute last thing he should be concerned with, but, still, he didn't shoot.

"But you see, Ranger Cooper, I know you, and I know your type. It's why I've managed to do as much damage as I have. Because you're all so honorable, or easy to buy off."

"Try to buy me off and see what happens."

The man chuckled, all ease and...something like

charm, though Vaughn wasn't at all charmed by it. Still, these were the most dangerous criminals to deal with, the ones without much at stake, except their own pride, or whatever was going on in their warped heads.

Of course he'd be charming and smooth, men like him were always charming and smooth. That was why people didn't suspect them. That was why he'd gotten this far. But also because reason and rational thinking wouldn't change their course. Nothing would. The man standing before him could do anything with zero remorse.

"But I'm not here for you," Callihan said with an elegant flick of the wrist. "I'm here for the woman. I have plans for the woman who thinks she can get her sister away from me."

Vaughn's entire body turned to ice. Even in the quiet desert, he didn't know if they were close enough for Natalie to hear that, but it was an admission. It was a certainty that Natalie's sister was with this man, and that he was after Natalie. For very specific reasons.

His finger itched to pull that trigger, to end this, now. Though they were still yards apart, Vaughn thought he saw Callihan's gaze drop to his gun.

"Lucky for me, Ranger Cooper, I don't need you. Quite frankly, wherever that woman is, I'll find her, but you'll be de—"

Vaughn pulled the trigger. The whistle of the shot,

followed by the man's piercing scream, were barely heard over the beating of his heart.

He'd purposefully shot for the man's weapon-wielding arm, and as Vaughn raced toward the dropped gun, Callihan started screaming for someone in Spanish.

Even though he knew Callihan was yelling for backup, which likely meant people with even larger weapons would be coming around that bend, he raced for the gun. Even though he knew he might have signed his death warrant, there was always a chance Callihan had only a few men with him, a chance Vaughn would be able to pick them off before…

But there was *no* chance if he didn't get to Callihan's weapon first.

Vaughn was so intent on reaching the weapon, and reaching Callihan that he didn't realize there were footsteps behind him.

"If you so much as touch that gun with a fingertip, I will shoot you, and I'm not a very good shot, so if I aim for your heart, I might just hit your head."

Vaughn skidded to a stop and looked back at Natalie, who was walking steadily toward them. She had the gun he'd taken from one of the men in the cabin trained on Callihan's writhing form.

The man merely smirked, his hand still reaching for the weapon, before Vaughn could pull his weapon, Natalie shot.

"That's the problem with women," Callihan all but

spat. "They can never shoot on tar—" She shot again, and this time Callihan howled.

Red bloomed at his stomach, and Natalie kept calmly walking forward, though now that she was close enough, Vaughn could see the way her arms were shaking. Callihan was screaming for someone named Rodriguez while he thrashed and moaned on the ground.

Right before Natalie and Vaughn reached Callihan's weapon, a large man stepped out from behind the curve of mountain. He was dressed all in black, had black sunglasses and black hair, with multiple guns strapped to him—all black. Everything about him was large and muscular and ominous.

"Shoot them!" Callihan screamed. "Kill them both. What are you doing?"

Vaughn didn't pull his trigger, and not just because the man didn't pull out a gun. The man was shockingly familiar. Not because he'd arrested him before, not because of anything criminal. He'd *trained* him a few years ago on undercover practices, though Vaughn couldn't come up with his name.

Callihan kept screaming at him to shoot, but the man didn't make a move to reach for a weapon. He walked calmly toward the three of them.

"Tell your woman to put down the gun," he said in Spanish, nodding toward Natalie, who was holding the gun trained on the man.

Vaughn glanced at her then, noting that everything

about her was shaking and pale and scared. But she was ready to take the shot.

"Put it down, Nat," he murmured.

"I won't let anyone kill us. Not now. Not when that man has my sister."

Callihan made a grab for his supposed henchman's leg piece, but the man easily kicked him away.

"Ma'am, I need you to put your weapon down," he said, steady and sure, making eye contact with Natalie. "I'm with the FBI. I've been working undercover for Callihan. I know where your sister is. She's…safe."

Natalie didn't just lower the gun, she dropped it. Then she sank to her knees, so Vaughn sank with her.

"Does this mean it's over?" she asked in a shaking, ragged voice.

"I think so," he said, stroking her hair. "I think so."

NATALIE SAT IN a truck squished between Vaughn and this…FBI agent. Vaughn and the man discussed the case, the particulars of the FBI's involvement and what the agent was allowed to disclose.

Natalie knew she should be listening, but everything was just a faded buzz. She couldn't seem to stop shaking, and all she could concentrate on was the fact the man in the back had become completely silent.

She'd shot him. Right in the stomach. He hadn't shut up though, he'd gone on and on as Vaughn and the agent, Jaime Alessandro, or so he said, had done the best to bandage Callihan, while also keeping him tied up.

Callihan had shouted terrible things about what he'd done to Gabby, but before he'd really gotten going, Agent Alessandro had knocked him out. Just a quick blow to the head. Then, they'd taped his mouth shut and thrown him into the truck he'd brought out to the desert.

All Natalie could concentrate on was how she'd tried to kill a man, and failed. She should be glad that she had failed, she should be glad that she hadn't apparently hit any internal organs, and that he would probably survive. She should be glad that he would stand trial.

All she felt was regret. She wished she would've killed him. For Gabby, for Vaughn, for herself. She wished he was dead, and she didn't know how to reconcile that with who she'd thought she was.

Despite being sandwiched between these two, strong, powerful men who were fighting for what was right and good, Natalie felt alone and vulnerable and scared. Which was something she didn't understand, either. Because it was over. This hell was over and they had survived, and with very little hurt.

But Gabby had been hurt. Gabby had survived eight years of that horrible man, and Natalie didn't know how… Now that it was over, *over*, she didn't know what on earth would possibly come next.

Jaime pulled into what appeared to be the national

park's ranger station. "If you stay put, I'll have them call for an ambulance, as well as call your precinct. We'll see if there's any word on the raid on Callihan's house, where your sister was."

Vaughn nodded stoically and Natalie just...stared. Word on the raid where her sister was. How was she supposed to respond to that? What was left? What was she supposed to do?

"Do you have questions about Gabby?"

She didn't glance at Vaughn, because she didn't know how to look at him. She didn't know how to look at the future. It was like dealing with all the fear and the threat had completely eradicated her ability to look beyond...anything. And now...it was all gone.

What did she do? "I don't know what to ask," she managed to say. Because she was numb and somehow still scared, and she didn't know why.

Vaughn didn't move or say anything for a long time, but eventually his hand rested on her clutched ones. He rubbed his warm strong palm over her tight, shaking hands.

It was warm, it was comfort. But when she looked up at him, his gaze was blank and straight ahead. Though he was offering her comfort, it was much more like the comfort he'd offered her that first night after the fire. There was something separate about it. Something stoic.

This wasn't the hug he'd offered her at the cabin, and that lack of...personal warmth made the frozen confusion inside her even worse. So she mimicked him. She didn't look at him anymore, she didn't move, she stared straight ahead.

When Agent Alessandro came back out, he explained that an ambulance would be waiting for them at the exit of the park, and he would have agents there who would confiscate Callihan's car. He would accompany Callihan to the hospital and keep him in FBI custody. Someone from the local police department would be there to escort Natalie and Vaughn to the airport, where the FBI would fly them back to Austin, after a medic checked Vaughn's wound.

He began to drive, explaining all sorts of things Natalie knew where important. What would be expected of her, what she would need to do and what questions she would need to answer before she was released.

But she couldn't concentrate. All she could think about was… "What about…"

"Your sister?" Agent Alessandro supplied for her.

"Yes."

"As I mentioned, the FBI is conducting raids on all of Callihan's properties while I had him…distracted, so to speak. The property your sister has been at is on that list. As I've been working my way up in his organization, I've released some of the women, but—"

She whipped her head to face him, this stranger who'd helped them. "But not my sister?"

Something in his face hardened. "She wouldn't go."

"Wouldn't go? What does that mean?"

"I'm afraid that's all I'm at liberty to say." His hands tensed and then released on the steering wheel. "But now that we have Callihan in custody, and with all of the information that I've gathered over my two years, there should be no doubt that the trafficking ring, and his entire business, will be gutted. You have my word on that Ms. Torres."

She didn't care about trafficking rings or business or anything like that, though she supposed she should. All she cared about was her sister, and why her sister could have been saved and wasn't.

Natalie pushed out a breath, doing her level best not to cry. Not yet. Not in front of Alessandro and Vaughn.

Only then did Natalie realize that Vaughn had released her hands. No comfort. No connection. Just an officer and a victim.

If she had any energy left, she might've felt bereft. She might've cried. And now… Now, all she wanted to do was go home. To be alone. To deal with the last week in the privacy of her own house…

Except she didn't have one, just a burned-out shell. She had so very little. She'd come out of this ordeal with her life, and she knew that was important.

Maybe in a few days, when the shock wore off and she saw Gabby again and held her and understood what had happened, she'd know how to feel.

Maybe it would take a few days for all the dust to settle, to hurt and grieve and *feel*. But for the time being, all she could do was feel numb.

Chapter Sixteen

Vaughn wasn't sure he'd ever felt so numb. Not even after his undercover mission years ago. He had never in his entire career left a case feeling so completely screwed up inside.

He'd stayed with Natalie through the debriefing. They'd been with each other through their medical evaluations. And yet, they'd said almost nothing to each other. They'd offered no reassuring glances, no comforting touches. The last time he'd touched her in any sort of personal capacity had been to put his hand on hers in the car.

He'd made sure to stop in that moment, because he'd realized he couldn't do this anymore. He couldn't possibly pretend that what they'd had in the cabin was real, and he couldn't give her false hope that he could be anything other than the man that he was. His job would always come first, someone else's safety would always come before his own.

How could he possibly tie another woman to him knowing where that ended?

It took days to get everything situated, questioned, figured out. When Natalie finally got to go home, or at least to her mother's home, he hadn't gone with her. She hadn't asked him to, and he hadn't offered. They had turned into strangers, and he felt like a part of him had simply…died.

It was so melodramatic he was concerned about his mental state, but he couldn't eradicate that feeling. He felt a darkness worse than after the failure of his marriage, more than his most difficult undercover missions. He'd lost some piece of himself, and he didn't know where to go to find it.

That's a lie, you know exactly what's missing.

He ruthlessly pushed that thought away as he talked to Agent Alessandro about the release of Natalie's sister. They would be reunited today. There was no reason Vaughn should be there. At this point, the case been taken over by the FBI, he'd released all files potentially related to The Stallion over to Alessandro and he'd…been expected to move on.

So, he had no reason, no right to be there when Natalie saw her sister again. In fact, even if they hadn't left things so oddly, it wouldn't be his place to be there. She deserved a private homecoming with her sister.

"You know, if you'd like to be there, I can see if I can make arrangements."

Vaughn ignored the tightness in his throat as he

responded to Jaime. "I'm not sure that would be… what they wanted."

"I can check, though, is what I'm offering."

"You'd been under for a long time, hadn't you?" Vaughn asked, changing the subject, turning it away from the numbness in his own chest.

The man on the other end of the line was silent for a while. "Yes, I had."

Jaime had been in the academy right after Vaughn had left undercover work, before he'd gotten on with the Rangers, and before Jaime would have gotten on with the FBI. Vaughn had taught a class on undercover work.

He didn't remember all the recruits, but he remembered the best ones. The ones with promise. Jaime had been one.

"Well, in all the tying up of loose ends, I don't think I thanked you. You sure made getting out of that situation a lot easier."

"I was just doing my job. You know how it goes."

"Yeah, I do." Too well. How often had he been doing his job and giving nothing else?

"I can ask if they want you to be there. Clearly…" Jaime trailed off, and Vaughn was glad for it. He wasn't looking for a heart-to-heart.

"I'm glad the case has been resolved. If there's anything else you need from me or the Rangers, you know where to—"

"You know, that class you taught back at the police

academy…it stuck with me. In fact, there was something you said that I'd always repeat to myself, when I needed to remember what I was doing this all for."

Something trickled through the numbness. Not a warmth exactly, some…sense of purpose. Some sense of accomplishment.

"You gave a big lecture about not losing your humanity, and being willing to bend your rigid moral obligations, without losing that human part of yourself. That was…by far the hardest part. Because I only had myself. At first."

"At first?"

"I guess it changes you, or should. Shifts your priorities."

"What does?"

Jaime was quiet again, a long humming stretch of seconds. "You know, finding…someone." He cleared his throat. "I just assumed you and Ms. Torres…"

He let that linger there. *You and Ms. Torres.*

"Well, anyway, I've got plenty to do. But, if you want me to pave the way for you, I can try."

"No. It's not my place."

"If you say so. I'll be in touch."

Vaughn hung up and scowled at the phone. Him and Natalie. Yeah, there'd been a thing, but it had been a thing born of fear and proximity. He'd known Jenny since he was fourteen. They'd dated for six years before they'd gotten married.

What disaster would he cause if he tried to build

something on a few days of being in the same cabin? No matter what pieces of themselves they'd shared, it was based on a foundation that hadn't just crumbled, but no longer existed.

I guess it changes you, or should. Shifts your priorities.

It had. Profoundly. Not Jenny or his love for her, but police work. It had altered him, and Jenny had never been satisfied with those changes.

He thought about that time, about how it had been easier, for both of them, to blame the job rather than admit there was a problem deep within themselves. How it had been far easier to blame some failing inside him than change it. Easier for her to blame his failings too.

He thought about those moments in the desert when he hadn't cared about all the moral choices he'd made as a police officer. When he hadn't cared about anything but Natalie's safety.

He pushed away from his desk. This was insanity. He scrubbed his hands over his hair, ready to throw himself into another case, into anything that wouldn't involve thinking about *him*. Or most especially *her*.

A knock sounded on his office door and Captain Dean stepped in. "Cooper," he greeted with a nod.

"Captain."

"I've just talked to a supervisor from the FBI, along with the officers from the gas station incident, and the other agencies involved in The Stallion case."

"Sir?"

"Everyone has what they need from you, so you're free to go."

"Go?"

"Vaughn, don't be dense. You've been working round-the-clock for nearly a week, you have an injury."

"Doctors and psych cleared me to do desk work."

"Go home. Sleep. Recharge. That's not a suggestion, Cooper. It's common sense."

Vaughn could have argued, he could have even pushed, but for what? In one FBI raid, half his cases had been wiped out. Families were being reunited, people were getting answers.

The crimes that had been committed would leave a mark, there were still people to find, but Vaughn had what he'd been on the brink of losing his mind over. Case closure.

He still felt dark and empty.

Because things *had* shifted. Natalie had given him light for the first time in a long time. A priority that existed beyond cases and police work. Someone who understood what it was to put someone else first, and the complexity of dealing with the unsolved.

Natalie *understood*, in ways most people probably couldn't. The unknowns, the toll it took, the complex emotions.

And that…that was a foundation that existed. A foundation that was stronger than any he could build with his own two hands. Possibly...possibly even a foundation that no one else could touch.

NATALIE WAS NOTHING but a bundle of nerves. Her mother sat stoically next to her in the hospital waiting room, and her grandmother was saying fervent prayers over her rosary.

The relationship between all three of them had been strained for so long, Natalie didn't know how to breach it now. For eight years she'd been certain her mother and grandmother's irritation and frustration with her obsession with Gabby's case had been a weakness.

It had been a betrayal. How dare they give up on Gabby?

But now...she realized they had all dealt with tragedy in the ways they could. They were all strong, independent women who had endured too much loss and hurt, and had dealt with it in the differing ways that suited them.

A nurse came through the door first, holding it open for a woman. Though she was nearly unrecognizable from the young woman Natalie remembered, it was too easy to see Dad's nose and Mom's pointed chin, and Natalie's own big eyes staring right back at her.

Natalie didn't remember getting to her feet, and she barely registered Grandma's loud weeping. Everything was centered in on…something indescribable. This woman who was her sister, and yet…not.

Her skin prickled with goose bumps, and she could scarcely catch a breath. Was she moving? She wasn't sure, but somehow she was suddenly in the middle of the room with…her sister.

Taller, older, *different*. And yet *hers*. She was flesh and blood and *here*. Natalie reached out, but she wasn't sure where to touch, or how.

"Nattie."

Even Gabby's voice was different, the light in her eyes, the way her mouth moved. Natalie was rendered immobile by all of it, crushed under the reality of eight years lost. Of the grief that swelled through her over losing the sister she'd known, that nickname, and all it would take to…

Her outstretched hand finally found purchase…because Gabby had grabbed it. Squeezed it in her own. It didn't matter that she wasn't the same person she'd been all those years ago, because Natalie wasn't the same person, either.

But they were still sisters. Blood. Connected.

"Say something," Gabby whispered, barely audible over the way Mom and Grandma were openly sobbing.

"I don't know…" What to say. What to do. Even as she'd thought about this moment for *years*, actually being here… "I'm so sorr—"

But Gabby shook her head and cupped Natalie's face with her hands. "No, none of that."

Which broke Natalie's thin grip on composure, and soon she was sobbing as well, but also holding on to Gabby, tight, desperate. Gabby held back, and though she didn't make a sound, Natalie could feel tears that weren't her own soak her shoulder.

"Mama, *Abuela*," Gabby's raspy voice ordered. "Come here."

Then all four of them were standing in the middle of a hospital waiting room, holding on too tightly, struggling to breathe through tears and hugs.

Gabby shook, something echoing all the way through her body so violently, Natalie could feel it herself.

"Are you all right? Do you need a doctor? I'll go get the nu—"

But Gabby held her close. "I'm all right, baby sister. I just can't believe it's real. You're all here."

"They…told you about…Daddy?"

Gabby swallowed, her chin coming up, everything about her hardening all over again. "The Stallion made sure I knew."

"But…"

Gabby shook her head. "No. Not today. Maybe not ever."

Natalie had to swallow down the questions, the need to pressure. The need to understand. She could want all she wanted, but Gabby would have to make the choices of what she told them herself. That was her right as survivor.

"One of us needs to get it together so we can drive home," their mother said, her hand shaking as she mopped up tears. Her other hand was a death grip around Gabby's elbow.

"I'm all right," Natalie assured them. "I'll drive. Right now. We're free to go. We're… Let's get out of here. And go home."

"Home," Gabby echoed, and Natalie couldn't begin to imagine what those words elicited for her sister. She couldn't begin to imagine…

Well, there'd be therapy for all of them, there'd be healing. One step at a time. The first step was getting out of this hospital.

But as they turned to leave the waiting room, someone entered, blocking the way.

It took Natalie a moment to place him, because the last time she'd seen Agent Alessandro he'd had much longer hair, a beard. He'd looked as menacing as The Stallion, if not more so.

He'd had a haircut and a shave and today looked every inch the FBI agent in his suit and sunglasses.

Gabby stopped and everything about her stiffened. "Agent Alessandro," Gabby greeted him coolly, and despite the tear tracks on her cheeks, she was shoulders-back strong, and Natalie couldn't begin to imagine what Gabby had endured to come out of this so…self-possessed, so strong.

"Ms. Torres." There was an odd twist to the FBI

agent's mouth, but his gaze moved from Gabby to her. "Ms.... Well, Natalie, I've got a message for you."

Gabby's grip tightened on her arm, but when she glanced at her sister, all Natalie saw was a blank stoicism.

"It's from the Texas Rangers Office."

It was Natalie's turn to grip, to stiffen. Because she heard "Texas Rangers" and she thought of Vaughn, she wanted to cry all over again for different reasons.

Anger. Regret. Loss. Confusion.

Mostly anger. She didn't have *time* for anger, all she had the time and energy for was Gabby.

Agent Alessandro held out a piece of paper and Natalie frowned at it. "They couldn't have called me? Sent an email?" she muttered, and though it was more rhetorical than an actual question, she glanced up at the agent.

His gaze was on Gabby again, and she was looking firmly away. They'd obviously had some interaction when Alessandro had been undercover, and Natalie could only assume it hadn't been a positive interaction.

She glanced at the piece of paper, a handwritten note of all things. She opened it and scowled at the scrawl.

Once you've settled in with your sister, there are a few pressing questions I'll need to ask you in person for full closure in the case.
Vaughn

Everything about it made her violently angry. That he'd written a *note*. That he couldn't have called and been a man about it. That he'd dared sign his name *Vaughn* instead of Ranger Cooper when that was *clearly* all he wanted to be.

She didn't want to get settled with her sister first. She wanted all of this to be over. Now.

"Agent Alessandro, would you be able to escort Gabby and my family home while I see to this?"

His eyebrows raised. "I'd love to be of service, but I doubt your sister..."

"Oh, no, please escort us, Mr. Alessandro. *I* don't have a problem with it in the least," Gabby replied, linking arms with Mama and Grandma. There was a battle light in Gabby's eyes that Natalie didn't recognize at all.

She almost stepped in, ready to put her own battle on the back burner. But Gabby's intense gaze turned to her. "Tie up loose ends, sissy. I want this over, once and for all."

"It will be," Natalie promised. It damn well would be.

Chapter Seventeen

Vaughn paced. He hadn't expected Natalie to come right away. He figured she'd want time with Gabby, and it would give him time to set up everything. But Jaime's clipped message had said that she was on her way. And it would probably be quick, despite the fact the hospital was on the other side of Austin.

"Can't lie that I don't mind seeing you like this," Bennet said companionably as Vaughn stalked his office.

"Thanks for your support," Vaughn muttered trying to figure out what the hell was trying to claw out of his chest. He'd expected time…possibly to talk himself out of the whole thing.

"You have all my support. In fact, I'm going to be the nice guy here and tell you that a simple apology probably won't cut it."

"You don't even know what the hell is going on." But apparently he was transparent because everyone seemed to know.

"You're right, I don't. But I know you're all tied up in knots, and I'd put money on the hot little hypnotist—"

At Vaughn's death glare, Bennet didn't even have the decency to shut up. The jackass laughed.

"Yeah, you're hooked."

"Define hooked," Vaughn growled.

"Going feral any time anyone even begins to mention her was the first hint."

Vaughn wanted to argue with him just for the sake of arguing with him, but Natalie was on her way over here, and he didn't have time. "So maybe something happened," he admitted through gritted teeth.

"And you screwed it up, of course. I'm not one to tell you what to do, Vaughn," Bennet began, all ease and comfortable cheerfulness.

When Vaughn snarled, Bennet laughed.

"Okay, maybe I don't mind telling you what to do all that much, but point of fact is, if you're trying to woo a woman, especially this particular woman, you're going to have to do something that I'm not sure you have in your arsenal."

"What's that?"

"Anything remotely romantic that includes putting your heart on the line. I think you're incapable of that."

"I'm not…incapable," Vaughn grumbled, but he was a little afraid that he was. Afraid that no matter what he decided about trying to start something with Natalie, something real, something that might turn into something long-term—a *chance*. All he wanted was a damn chance.

But Bennet was still yammering on. "Since you don't have flowers, I'd figure out a romantic gesture or two."

Vaughn might have physically recoiled at the phrase *romantic gesture*.

"Probably something she'd never expect you to do, but you do because you want her."

Damn it. He *hated* that Bennet was right. Because he'd screwed this up, worse than he'd screwed up his marriage. Because the past few days of treating Natalie like a stranger at best… He'd known it was wrong. He'd felt it, in his bones, and the only thing he'd had to do to fix it was *speak*. Reach out. Put a little bit of pride on the line.

But he hadn't. So now that he was doing it, now that he was done being a little wimp, he had to not just put it all on the line, but offer it up wrapped in a damn bow.

"I need an interrogation room, and no interruptions. Can you make that happen?"

Bennet grinned, but he didn't give Vaughn any more crap. "On it. Good luck, buddy."

Yeah, luck. Strange all Vaughn could feel was an impending sense of dread.

But no matter how much dread he felt, no matter how little he knew about putting his pride or his shoddy heart on the line, he knew that the minute he saw her, that's exactly what he had to do.

NATALIE BURST INTO the Texas Rangers offices, and after jumping through all the hoops she had to jump through to get to the floor with Vaughn's office, Ranger Stevens was there to greet her. "Ms. Torres. It's good to see you under better circumstances."

"*Are* they better circumstances?" Which was flippant, because of course they were better. Her house hadn't burned down today, and she'd been reunited with her sister.

But she was angry, and she wanted to fling her anger at everyone who got in her way. Every second she was away from Gabby, she was going to be angry.

"Follow me," Ranger Stevens offered, sounding far too amused.

She followed him, pausing at the door to an interrogation room. It was the interrogation room where she'd all but signed Herman's death warrant. Where she'd set everything into motion, because she hadn't been able to keep her mouth shut.

She wasn't foolish enough to think that had put *everything* into motion. Obviously the FBI had had its own thing going on. It was happenstance she had gotten mixed up in it.

It was all *too* much, and Vaughn—the man who'd been *silent* for *days*—had the gall to send her a note— a *note*!—to answer more questions.

She ignored the part where she'd been silent too. Because she was afraid if she let go of any of her rage, she'd simply fall apart.

"He's waiting."

She scowled at Stevens, but then she entered the room on that last wave of fury.

Vaughn stood with his back to her, his palms pressed to the interrogation table. It hurt to look at him. To look at him and not touch him. It seemed that seeing Gabby this morning had broken that dam of feeling that she'd been hiding behind since she'd shot the man who'd kidnapped Gabby.

She'd been numb for days, but now, all she could do was *feel*. All she could seem to do was hurt. She was afraid she was going to cry, but she swallowed it down as best she could.

"You summoned."

Vaughn turned, and she wasn't prepared for those gray-blue eyes, the way the sight of his body and mouth trying to curve in a smile slammed through her.

She wanted to hug him and to cry into his shoulder. She wanted *him*.

But despite that a world of emotion *seemed* to glitter blue in those smoky eyes, he merely gestured to a seat at the table. "Have a seat, Ms. Torres."

"I think you're damn lucky I've taken a vow of antiviolence, because I'd as soon shove that seat up *your* seat as sit in it."

She had clearly caught him off guard with that, and she felt a surge of victory with all that anger. Let him take a step back. She wanted him to react.

"Natalie, just sit down and—"

"Go to hell." Which was probably cruel, but she wanted to be cruel, because maybe if she was, this could be over, and she could move on. She whirled toward the door.

"I was going to let you hypnotize me."

She whirled back, somehow every sentence he uttered making the violent thing inside of her larger. "What?"

"It's supposed to be romantic," he returned, clearly irritated she wasn't falling into line.

"What the hell is romantic about me hypnotizing you? You can't tell me how you feel unless I put you under?"

"You gave me a whole lecture about people being unable to give information under hypnotism unless they want to, and I'm trying to show you how *willing* I am to—"

"Then just *say* it!"

"I love you."

They both stood in stunned silence for Natalie wasn't sure how long. She clutched her hands at her chest and tried to…process that. Meanwhile Vaughn stood stock-still, his eyes a little wide as if he was shocked by his own words.

"I don't…believe in a lot of…" Vaughn rubbed

his palm across his jaw and then took a step toward her. "Natalie, I fell in love with you. Your strength, your dedication." He swore. "And I thought that'd go away, or dull, or… I don't want to *fail* someone else. I'm so sick of feeling like I failed, and I just wanted to show you that I'd do it anyway."

"Fail?" she asked incredulously.

"Try!"

"Oh." He loved her, and he wanted to try. He was trying to be…*romantic*. Vaughn Cooper. For her.

"Will you sit now?"

"No."

His eyebrows drew together, but before he could be too confused over her refusal, she found the courage to do what she'd wanted to do the moment she'd stepped in the room.

She moved into him, wrapping her arms around him, holding him through the ragged exhale he let out. "Nat—"

"I love you too," she whispered fiercely. Because that was such a better emotion to focus on than anger. *That* was what she should have taken away from this morning and being reunited with Gabby, not feeling *anything… Love.* Hope. Faith.

"I wasn't sure… I'm not sure I know how to go from the most important thing to me being your safety—and me *keeping* you safe, to you just…being safe. How does…any of this work?"

She pulled back a little and tried to smile, but a

few tears slipped out instead. She could tell it bothered him, but he didn't rush to stop her. No, for all Vaughn's gruff, by-the-book protector conventions, he always seemed to give her the space she needed to work it out.

And hold her through it if she needed.

"My life is literally burned to the ground, and I have a sister who's been held prisoner for eight years finally back in it. I don't know how *any* of this works, but I just guess you…figure it out."

"Together?"

"We make a pretty good team."

He wiped away one of her tears, his rough thumb a welcome texture against her cheek, his mouth gently curved, that *love* shining so clearly in his eyes. "We do," he agreed, his voice rough and…true.

Because Vaughn didn't lie, and he didn't sugarcoat. This man, who understood obsessions and failures, violence and the absence of it. How to keep her safe, how to give her space.

They made a *wonderful* team, and Natalie was certain that's exactly what they'd continue to be.

* * * * *

REQUEST YOUR FREE BOOKS!
2 FREE NOVELS PLUS 2 FREE GIFTS!

Ⓗ **HARLEQUIN**®

INTRIGUE

BREATHTAKING ROMANTIC SUSPENSE

YES! Please send me 2 FREE Harlequin® Intrigue novels and my 2 FREE gifts (gifts are worth about $10). After receiving them, if I don't wish to receive any more books, I can return the shipping statement marked "cancel." If I don't cancel, I will receive 6 brand-new novels every month and be billed just $4.74 per book in the U.S. or $5.49 per book in Canada. That's a savings of at least 12% off the cover price! It's quite a bargain! Shipping and handling is just 50¢ per book in the U.S. and 75¢ per book in Canada.* I understand that accepting the 2 free books and gifts places me under no obligation to buy anything. I can always return a shipment and cancel at any time. Even if I never buy another book, the two free books and gifts are mine to keep forever.

182/382 HDN GH3D

Name _____ (PLEASE PRINT)

Address _____ Apt. #

City _____ State/Prov. _____ Zip/Postal Code

Signature (if under 18, a parent or guardian must sign)

Mail to the **Reader Service:**
IN U.S.A.: P.O. Box 1867, Buffalo, NY 14240-1867
IN CANADA: P.O. Box 609, Fort Erie, Ontario L2A 5X3
**Are you a subscriber to Harlequin® Intrigue books
and want to receive the larger-print edition?
Call 1-800-873-8635 or visit www.ReaderService.com.**

* Terms and prices subject to change without notice. Prices do not include applicable taxes. Sales tax applicable in N.Y. Canadian residents will be charged applicable taxes. Offer not valid in Quebec. This offer is limited to one order per household. Not valid for current subscribers to Harlequin Intrigue books. All orders subject to credit approval. Credit or debit balances in a customer's account(s) may be offset by any other outstanding balance owed by or to the customer. Please allow 4 to 6 weeks for delivery. Offer available while quantities last.

Your Privacy—The Reader Service is committed to protecting your privacy. Our Privacy Policy is available online at www.ReaderService.com or upon request from the Reader Service.

We make a portion of our mailing list available to reputable third parties that offer products we believe may interest you. If you prefer that we not exchange your name with third parties, or if you wish to clarify or modify your communication preferences, please visit us at www.ReaderService.com/consumerschoice or write to us at Reader Service Preference Service, P.O. Box 9062, Buffalo, NY 14240-9062. Include your complete name and address.

Nick and Kody Cameron had passed briefly, like
proverbial ships in the night, but he hadn't had the least
problem recognizing her today. He knew her, because
they had both paused to stare at one another at the pub.

Instant attraction? Definitely on his part, and he could
have sworn on hers, too.

If Dakota Cameron saw his face, if she gave any
indication that she knew him, and knew that he was an
FBI man...

They'd both be dead.

And it didn't help the situation that she was battle
ready—ready to lay down her life for her friends.

Then again, there should have been a way for him to
stop this. If it hadn't been for the little boy who had been
taken...

Kody Cameron had a ledger opened before her, but she
was looking at him. Quizzically.

It seemed as if she suspected she knew him but couldn't figure out from where.

"You're not as crazy as the others," she said softly. "I can sense that about you. But you need to do something to stop this. That treasure he's talking about has been missing for years and years. God knows, maybe it's in the Everglades, swallowed up in a sinkhole. You don't want to be a part of this—I know you don't. And those guys are lethal. They'll hurt someone…kill someone. This is still a death-penalty state, you know. Please, if you would just—"

He found himself walking over to her at the desk and replying in a heated whisper, "Just do what he says and find the damned treasure. Lie if you have to! Find something that will make Dillinger believe that you know where the treasure is. Give him a damned map to find it. He won't think twice about killing people, but he won't kill just for the hell of it. Don't give him a reason."

"You're not one of them. You have to stop this. Get away from them," she said.

She was beautiful, earnest, passionate. He wanted to reassure her. To rip off his mask and tell her that law enforcement was on it all.

But that was impossible, lest they all die quickly.

He had to keep his distance and keep her, the kidnapped child and the others in the house alive.

Don't miss LAW AND DISORDER
by New York Times *bestselling author Heather Graham,
available February 2017 wherever
Harlequin® Intrigue books and ebooks are sold.*

www.Harlequin.com

READERSERVICE.COM

Manage your account online!

- Review your order history
- Manage your payments
- Update your address

> ### We've designed the Reader Service website just for you.

Enjoy all the features!

- Discover new series available to you, and read excerpts from any series.
- Respond to mailings and special monthly offers.
- Connect with favorite authors at the blog.
- Browse the Bonus Bucks catalog and online-only exculsives.
- Share your feedback.

Visit us at:

ReaderService.com

HARLEQUIN®

A *Romance* FOR EVERY MOOD™

JUST CAN'T GET ENOUGH?

Join our social communities
and talk to us online.

You will have access to the latest
news on upcoming titles and special
promotions, but most importantly,
you can talk to other fans about your
favorite Harlequin reads.

Harlequin.com/Community

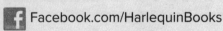

Facebook.com/HarlequinBooks

Twitter.com/HarlequinBooks

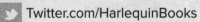

Pinterest.com/HarlequinBooks

Turn your love of reading into rewards you'll love with

Harlequin My Rewards

**Join for FREE today at
www.HarlequinMyRewards.com**

Earn **FREE BOOKS** of your choice.

Experience **EXCLUSIVE OFFERS** and contests.

Enjoy **BOOK RECOMMENDATIONS**
selected just for you.

PLUS! Sign up now
and get **500** points
right away!

Earn
FREE
REWARDS
Join!
Today!
HarlequinMyRewards.com

MYR16R

THE WORLD IS BETTER WITH

Romance

Harlequin has everything from contemporary, passionate and heartwarming to suspenseful and inspirational stories.

Whatever your mood, we have a romance just for you!

Connect with us to find your next great read, special offers and more.

f /HarlequinBooks

🐦 @HarlequinBooks

www.HarlequinBlog.com

www.Harlequin.com/Newsletters

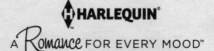

HARLEQUIN

A *Romance* FOR EVERY MOOD™

www.Harlequin.com